BREATHLESS

TWISTED FAIRY TALES

ENCHANTED FABLES: BOOK ONE

MEGAN LINSKI

For all my author friends.

CHAPTER ONE

ADRIAN

T t was a green fin… too large to belong to any fish. Only a few feet below the surface, a merman swam.

He had red hair and blue eyes, with a rugged chin and a devious smile. His warm ivory skin contrasted with the brightness of his tail, which was green in color, and translucent in the light breaking through the water, scales gleaming like gemstones. The end of his tail drifted downward in the water, wavering back and forth like a proud banner.

A bag hung around his bare chest, one made of tightly-knit netting. He was darting around the remains of a recent shipwreck, a yacht that had sunk in last week's storm. In his left hand he carried a golden trident, which he used to poke through the shipwreck's ruins.

A manatee floated beside him, swimming as quickly as she could keep up. She was young, and very cute, but her whiskers wrinkled in irritation as she watched her friend dive within the mess of the shipwreck.

"Adrian, we shouldn't be here," she worried. The manatee swam anxiously back and forth, twiddling her fins at her sides. "It's too close to the shore."

"Moona, you worry too much. The humans aren't going to see you and faint," he said with a laugh.

The merman was carefree, and careless. He knew as much, but it didn't bother him. He wasn't a king yet. Most knew him as Prince Adrian, son of Poseidon, heir to the sea.

To Moona, he was just a pain in her very large rear.

"*I'm* okay. I'm a *manatee*. They know I exist," Moona grumbled.

Adrian didn't hear her. Moona swam as close to Adrian as she could, but got stuck in a round doorway. She wiggled and writhed, but she couldn't get out.

"Adrian, help!" Moona cried.

Adrian rolled his eyes and swam toward Moona. He rammed his shoulder against her backside and pushed.

Moona popped through the doorway and smashed into one of the yacht's bedrooms. Adrian tumbled after her and smacked his head into a headboard.

"Ow," Adrian said, and he rubbed his temple. "Really, Moona?"

"I told you I was going on a diet. I didn't say it was working," Moona snapped back. "Stop taking me into places you know I won't fit."

Adrian wasn't listening. Something had caught his eye. He moved off the bed and swam downward.

"Look at this." From beneath a blanket Adrian pulled out a square, plastic object. He shook it and smiled, playing with the buttons.

"It's a video game console." He grinned. "I can't believe I'm lucky enough to find one of these."

"It's not going to work underwater," Moona said, poking it with her nose.

"Doesn't matter. It's still cool." Adrian put the console in his bag and continued searching the room. He took various objects; a designer shirt, an old journal, a fork and knife.

Moona swam up to the surface for more air. When she came back down, she was grumpier than before.

"Adrian, we really have to go," Moona said. This time, she sounded truly worried. "Your father will send people to look for us if we don't head back."

Adrian pocketed the fork inside his bag. "All right. Let's go."

They swum out of the wreckage and away from the yacht. Adrian was swimming so close to the surface the tips of his tail rose and fell with the waves. Moona did a smacking motion with her lips that gave away her anxiety.

"Rules were made to be broken," Adrian said teasingly, and he wiggled his tail out of the water. It made Moona wince.

"It's not about that. I don't care about rules. I care about *you*," Moona replied. "If your father was to find out…"

"Dad isn't going to find out." Adrian rolled his eyes. "I've been outside the city thousands of times without his permission. What makes you think he's suddenly going to wise up to what I'm doing *now*?"

"It's not just Poseidon. Humans are scary. Who knows what they'd do if they knew merpeople exist?" Moona questioned.

"Humans aren't that bad," Adrian said. "They wouldn't hurt us."

"Oh, yeah? How can you be sure?"

Adrian dodged the question, because he wasn't sure of the answer. "You know, we wouldn't be friends if I didn't come close to the surface so often," Adrian teased.

That shut Moona up. Manatees usually stuck to rivers, bays, and the coastline. They didn't wander far out to sea often… and Adrian's adventurous nature was the reason they had met in the first place.

Adrian turned downward. Waiting by a large collection of coral was his seahorse, Celer.

Celer was larger than Adrian, and had the body composition of a regular seahorse, but his color was spectacular. The creature's body was turquoise, and he had a dipped nose with two large ears on the top of his head. Celer's mane waved as soft tendrils in the water, appearing brilliant.

"Hey, boy," Adrian whispered. "Look what we found."

Adrian pulled out a piece of seaweed from the bag. He fed it to Celer, who ate it happily.

Adrian climbed astride Celer's back, sitting at an angle with his fin off to the side.

"We'd better get back. The party's already started, I bet," Moona quipped.

Adrian scowled. "Oh, *goody*." His nineteenth birthday— a day he'd dreaded the arrival of since last year.

"Cheer up, Adrian. You get to pick out your queen from a bunch of babes. What's not to love?" Celer whinnied.

Adrian made a face. He wasn't ready to get married, even if it was to a *babe*. The minute he said *I do* to a mermaid, all his exploring would be brought to an instant halt. He might as well be handing his life away.

A shadow from above caught his attention. There was a boat sailing above them. It was around thirty feet long, a tour boat that tourists took out on the water in search of dolphins or whales. Adrian's curiosity peaked.

"We should go up there and get a glimpse of the leg-walkers," he mused. "What do you say, Moona?"

Moona had gotten distracted and was happily chewing on a spare bit of seaweed she'd found in Adrian's bag. She didn't care.

Adrian shook his head and got off of Celer to swim upward. "Whatever."

The seaweed fell out of Moona's mouth when she realized he was approaching the boat. "Adrian. *Adrian*!"

Adrian wasn't listening. Moona anxiously weaved back and forth, unsure of what to do.

But Moona wouldn't leave Adrian's side, not for anything, so she paddled up to her friend as quickly as she could and joined him at the surface.

Adrian poked his head out of the water, and Moona's nose appeared beside him. He remained silent as he crept up to the tour ship, trying not to make noise.

Adrian had always been fascinated by humans. He wasn't sure why. There was just something about the leg-walkers that was special to him... like their technology. Humans were constantly evolving and on the move, discovering the next big thing.

The city of Aquatica never changed, and neither did merpeople. Adrian didn't think his kind had any advancements or excitement since the Middle Ages.

But humans... there was always something thrilling to see and do on land.

A girl was talking at the head of the boat. She was the tour guide. Though she was supposed to appear chipper and bright, she sounded bored.

"And over there is one of the biggest coral reefs

in the region," she said monotonously— like she was reading from an old book, and not explaining one of the area's local treasures.

Adrian liked the way her voice sounded. He wanted a closer look. He swam a little nearer, and Moona held her breath.

"Look, a manatee!" someone shouted, and everyone ran to the side of the boat that Adrian was under. He went to slip underwater, but something saw him first.

Someone.

It was the tour guide. The girl. Her eyes had flickered downward, and she'd spotted Adrian.

Their gazes connected for a singular moment, a millisecond. It was all Adrian needed to burn her shocked expression into his mind forever. She had green eyes, like the shallow waves upon the shore, and blonde hair that was wavy, like it'd just dried after she'd gotten out of the sea. Her skin was tan, as if she couldn't help but soak up the sun. Her round lips curved as he took in her long legs and shapely hips.

He liked what he saw.

Moona shoved him, and he startled out of his reverie. Adrian dove downward before anyone else saw, giving the girl a glimpse of his tail.

Adrian swam as fast as he could. He spun onto Celer's back and said, "Get us out of here, boy."

Poor Moona struggled to keep up. By the time the boat was out of sight, she'd had to go back up for air again.

Adrian's head was spinning long after the sight of the boat was gone. He couldn't get the image of the girl out of his head. He wished he knew her name.

"What. The. *Hell*," Moona moaned. She slapped her flippers against her sides. "This is bad. This is really bad."

"It's no big deal, Moona," Adrian said in irritation. Why had he brought her along?

If it weren't for Moona, you'd have been pulled onto that boat and be in a lab by now, he reminded himself. He'd been stuck frozen in that girl's stare. A fisherman could've run a harpoon through his middle and he doubt he would've felt it.

She was… wow. Incredible.

"Hello! Adrian!" Moona poked him again. "This is serious! A human saw you! This is a big deal!"

Adrian tried to shake it off. "Humans have seen merpeople before. That's why they have stories about them."

"Yes, but they have phonies now! *Technology*. If they get a video of you on one of their phonies and post it to the Intraweb, you're done for!"

"It's called a phone, Moona, not phonies. I'm not even going to correct you on what you call the Internet. And also, humans make up a lot of things now. Everything in their world is fake. They would never believe a story about a merman, anyway."

His father *would* find out, however… someway, somehow. And what would happen after… total tidal wave catastrophe.

"Calm down, Moona. You heard Adrian. Nothing happened," Celer replied coolly. "Now let's get back to the palace, so Adrian can go check out those *babes*."

Celer, apparently, was obsessed with babes.

Moona let it drop and said nothing more. They swam back to Aquatica in silence. Adrian kept replaying what had happened in his head. Though it'd only been a moment, staring into the girl's eyes had seemed like a lifetime.

Though it wasn't satisfying, and it wasn't enough. If he didn't have obligations, he'd swim after the boat, and use his magic to go on land for a few hours and look for the girl, before the sea forced him back into the water.

It wasn't meant to be, though.

His destiny lied in Aquatica, with his merpeople. He belonged under the sea, not on land.

Adrian desperately wished that would change.

CHAPTER TWO

ISA

Isa really hated her summer job.

She didn't need the money — her dad gave her everything she needed — but it wasn't about that. Sure, she would've preferred to earn her own income, but at a job that she chose for *herself*… not one her father picked out for her, one that came tied with promises and obligations.

Being a guide on her uncle's dolphin tour boat wasn't exactly a bad gig. She enjoyed looking out for ocean creatures, and it had been what had gotten her into the Marine Biology program at the local university. They wanted people with experience, and Isa, having grown up around whales, manatees, and coral reefs, was their perfect applicant.

And besides… she was out on the water. There was nothing Isa loved more than being on the sea.

She'd spent more time in the ocean than on land, that was for sure. She was practically a fish herself.

But— and it was a big *but*— her dad had *told* her this was what she was going to do this summer, and she wasn't given a choice. He didn't even ask her if she wanted to. *That's* why Isa hated it.

Her dad seemed to forget that she wasn't in the Navy, like he was. He couldn't always dictate what she wanted to do.

Except he could. He still paid her college tuition, and without him funding her education, she'd never finish her degree. So she did as she was told, and that meant every Saturday for five hours, she was on a tour boat. It was made slightly more bearable that she had a second job, an internship at the local aquarium— something she actually *enjoyed* doing.

Her dad didn't need to know about the second job. He wouldn't approve, and Isa didn't like the idea of getting another lecture about her future.

Every Saturday, Isa gave the same two tours, gave the same old speech, and answered the same old questions.

However, this time was different.

Isa had *seen* someone in the water, and yes, she was certain it was a someone. It was a boy… at first, she'd thought he was a tourist who'd fallen out of the boat, but that thought changed when she looked into his eyes. She knew from the moment thier gazes had connected she'd never seen him before in her life. He was different— and yet, he was just like her.

She didn't know *how* she knew that, but she was ultimately convinced that the two of them were the same, and nothing anyone could say would change her mind. Their souls connected on impact. She could feel it, and she bet he could, too.

But then the boy panicked, and before she could say anything more to him, he'd dived. Isa had expected to see legs, but she didn't.

She saw a *fishtail.*

Isa convinced herself she was crazy. She had to be seeing things. There was no boy in the water. There couldn't be. A triathlon swimmer couldn't keep up with the waves and the undertow so far away from the shoreline... not for long, anyway. They'd drown. Unless the boy had hidden away in the boat somehow... which was unlikely... there was no such person out here. Her eyes were playing tricks on her.

Isa dropped off the tourists at the dock. She tapped her fingers on the steering wheel of the boat before backing it up and whirling it around, into the ocean.

She steered the boat out to the same spot she saw the boy. She dropped the anchor, then pulled off her shorts and tank top.

Isa always wore a bikini under her clothes. She didn't see the point in wearing anything else when she'd always end up in the ocean at one point or another in the day.

There was a harpoon on the boat. It was an antique, one her uncle only used to exaggerate fishing stories. It had been an old weapon to kill sharks and whales hundreds of years ago. Isa considered taking it with her to defend herself, just in case there was something scary down there, until she berated herself for being crazy. Unless it was a shark, she really had nothing to fear.

Isa fastened goggles to her face, then dove in. She held her breath as she swam in wide strokes, not really sure what she was looking for... if anything.

In each direction she looked, there was nothing but an expanse of blue water. She couldn't even see any fish. Isa dove down farther, but she didn't accomplish anything. She was fighting the current, and getting tired. Isa returned to the boat before she became too exhausted, and before the sea claimed her for its own.

Disappointed, Isa climbed back onto the boat. *I don't know what I was thinking. I'm nuts.*

Isa closed her eyes and pictured the boy again. She could still see him... water dangling from his lashes, and soft waves in his red hair she could imagine running her hands though.

Cut it out, Isa. He's not a Disney prince. He doesn't even exist.

She must've been out in the sun for too long. Or she was so pissed at her dad she was imagining running off with some hot dude just to say *screw you.*

Isa guided the boat back to shore. She docked

her uncle's boat at the marina, then once it was secure, headed to the office and got her longboard.

Her dad had bought her a car, but Isa enjoyed skating around Coral Bay more than she did driving.

Her father didn't like it when she went skateboarding... he thought it made her look like a punk. Isa enjoyed the exercise. She had too much energy. Everyday, it felt like she was going to jump out of her skin. Working out made that feeling go away, at least for a little bit.

Isa put her helmet on and glided down the street on her board. She did some ollies and skimmed down some stair rails, then took a few minutes to do some jumps at the skate park before she realized how late it was. She hurried home from there, and threw her longboard in the garage once she got to the three-story stucco.

"Dad, I'm home!" She loped into the massive, open-concept kitchen, but he wasn't there. The only person around was their maid, Paola.

"He's not here, *chica*," Paola said when she noticed Isa poking around the too-large rooms, all pristine in appearance. It was as if the house was a living magazine, and not a place where people resided. "He's still at work."

"Do you know when he'll be home, Paola?" Isa asked. She breathed a sigh of relief that was accompanied by disappointment. He was supposed to be here so she could fry grouper tonight... his favorite. He'd been gone since five that morning. Isa knew, because she was up at that time and hadn't been able to sleep.

She could never sleep these days.

Paola shook her head. "No. But I took the fish out of the freezer, just in case."

Isa's lips downturned, and her stomach rumbled. "It's okay. I'll wait up for him."

"Don't wait too long, *chica*. Remember to eat." Paola kissed her forehead while she gathered her purse. Isa wanted to beg her to stay so she wouldn't be alone again in this big house, but Paola had her own family to go home to, and she was a big girl. She could take care of herself.

Isa busied herself with homework at the island in the kitchen, looking out the window every few minutes.

When her father finally pulled into the driveway at eight, Isa jumped up from her chair and went to start battering the fish. It was soggy in the sink.

Colson walked into the house with a fast food bag, and Isa froze.

"Hello, Ria," he said, using her old nickname from when Isa was a child. It irritated her, because it was a shortened version of her mother's name, and Isa didn't wish to be reminded of her... the woman she could never compete with.

Her father plopped a bag on the counter. "I stopped for dinner."

Take-out again. Oh well. At least it was something to eat.

"I… was supposed to make dinner for you," Isa trailed off. "Remember?"

Her father's face was blank. "Oh. Sorry, honey. I got you a salad."

He'd forgotten. She'd left a note this morning *and* texted him. How could he have forgotten *again?*

"It's okay," she said, and she threw the fish back in the freezer. "It's too late to cook, anyway."

Her father joined her at the island. He started in on his burger and fries while she chewed her salad dutifully.

"How was your day at work?" she asked, wanting to break the conversation.

"Okay." He shrugged. "Nothing out of the ordinary. Typical duties."

Being a Navy Admiral, her father couldn't talk much about what he did. Isa knew it wasn't his fault, but sometimes, it made her feel like he didn't want to talk to her.

"There was someone in the water today," she blurted out. She wanted to say something to get her father's attention, even if it was dumb.

"Not unusual. It is Florida. Lots of people in the water," he said noncommittally.

"No, I mean, it was a boy. He…"

Her father briefly looked up, and she lost her courage. She shook her head. "Never mind."

"You know, the Seaside Ball is coming up," her father mentioned — for the hundredth time in a row — and her stomach dropped. "Have you gotten your dress yet? You'll need a pretty one when they crown you Coral Queen."

"I don't know if I'm going to win, Dad," Isa mumbled. "Can't we drop it?"

"I don't see why you wouldn't win." He wiped his mouth. "You're the most beautiful girl in town. The obvious choice."

Isa was careful with her reply. Being crowned Coral Queen at the annual Seaside Ball was every girl's dream in Coral Bay. Many dreamed about it from the time they were three years old. Girls had fought over the position before— even sabotaged each other for it— but whoever won the crown was determined by popular vote.

Isa knew she was a shoe-in for the crown. Despite being a bit of an introvert, she'd been elected homecoming queen *and* prom queen in high school. For some unknown reason, she'd been popular, and everyone at school loved her.

She couldn't figure out why, except she knew people thought her pretty, and it helped that her dad was one of the richest and most powerful people in town. Because of it, everyone tried to suck up to her and get on her good side.

Yep. She played the part of the queen bee well. But it was all a distraction... a mask... a role she took as an actress that wasn't her. Isa didn't want to be Coral Queen any more than she wanted to claw her eyes out. Isa wanted the crown to go to a girl who actually wanted it... someone who deserved it... someone who wasn't a fake.

In other words, not her. For that shell-shaped crown to be placed on her head would be the cherry on top of her ice-cream sundae of shitty lies and poor cover-ups.

If people knew who she really was inside… well, they wouldn't even come *near* her. Forget about being Coral Queen.

It wasn't just about her peers. Her dad had *very* specific roles and rules for women. Isa didn't fit into any of them, and as such, was a big disappointment to him. As he constantly reminded her.

"I don't know," she said. "I… uh… don't want to get my hopes up."

"Your mother won the Coral Queen crown," Colson said. "It would be great for you to follow in her footsteps."

Isa didn't know why her dad cared so much about what her mother had done. She'd left, after all. He was still in love with a ghost, a phantom who was living several states away with a much younger, and most likely more affectionate, man. Isa hadn't spoken to her in years.

"Maybe." She played with her fork. Though she'd been starving when her father got here, she was no longer hungry.

"I'll leave money on the table tomorrow. You can go shopping for your dress in the morning," her dad said. He finished eating and cleaned up the wrappings. He threw away the empty bag and went up to his suite to take a shower without so much as a goodnight.

Isa bit her lip and tried to shove the feelings down. She hated whenever her father brought up her mother in conversation, which was often. Paola had been around far longer and been far more of a mom than Isa's biological mother ever had, but her father never acknowledged that. Paola had helped her learn to walk, changed her diapers, and put together all of Isa's birthday parties, but for Colson, it wasn't enough. To him, Paola was just *the help*.

Her father's words made clear that if Isa wasn't chosen for Coral Queen, she'd fail to measure up to her mother, which would be unforgivable.

Isa *could not* handle that. She really wanted to skip the stupid Seaside Ball altogether, and take a stand on who she really was to her father. But part of her wanted to win the crown, and make her dad proud of her... just this once. He wasn't proud of her when she'd graduated as valedictorian, or when she'd gotten into the Marine Biology program. Maybe winning some sexist crown and pretending to be a real princess for a day would finally make him love her.

Isa threw her half-eaten salad away and kicked the trash can. Screw this. She was going out. She needed her board. She needed to ride the waves. She needed to be *free*.

Isa texted Harbor and Shelly and told them to meet her down by the beach, at the usual spot. She zipped up her wetsuit and grabbed her surfboard, careful to avoid the automatic lights so her dad wouldn't catch her sneaking out.

Like he'd give a damn anyway.

Isa skated down the street. A few raindrops sprinkled down from the clouds that had covered the area, and the sky gave an ominous rumble, but Isa ignored both.

She was going surfing.

CHAPTER THREE

ADRIAN

Adrian was seriously bored at his birthday party.

The underwater palace was decked out in all its finest. The silver towers were wrapped in gold and aquamarine, the colors that were picked for Adrian's herald the day he was born.

He was made to wear a very stuffy shirt in the same colors, some- thing that would make his father happy but that he hated. Celer was flirting with mares in the stables, and Moona stayed outside — she didn't like crowds.

The great hall was already swarming with merpeople. The hall was suited to fit at least five hundred merpeople, but Adrian could swear there were double that packed into the space. The band was playing some sort of jazzy underwater song that Adrian had heard a thousand times. It was like the tune was all they knew.

This party sucked. Adrian would've been happy with some classic hard rock, blared as loud as it could go, and booze.

Lots and lots of booze.

He didn't really need to drink, as the ocean provided what he needed, but he'd snuck off to go onshore plenty of times to have a few beers. He didn't like how it made him feel, but he *did* like how it made him forget.

Most nineteen-year olds had massive parties where stuff would get broken and no one would remember what happened later. All of Adrian's birthdays were the same from the moment he could remember them. Balls, dances, civil affairs. The only people his age that came were children of high society merpeople. The rest were his father's friends.

Adrian surpassed the tall piles of gifts that were next to his throne. He wasn't much of a material guy. He never was interested in merfolk presents, anyway. He preferred antiques from on land.

A herald called out over the noise. "Mermen and merladies, please applaud for the arrival of King Poseidon, King of the Sea, Ruler of the Ocean, and his wife, Queen Ianthe, Mistress of the Waves, Protector of the Depths."

Poseidon wasn't anything to scoff at. He was brawny, with light green skin that was scaly all over, and a tail that was larger than some mermen were tall. He had long black hair that billowed out behind him, and he carried a bejeweled trident that Adrian struggled to lift.

Adrian's mother clung dutifully to her husband's arm. Ianthe was tall, thin, and gorgeous. She had red hair that was braided into a crown around her head, and was wearing a lavender dress to compliment her purple tail. She gave Adrian a kind smile as they approached.

"My son." Poseidon took his arm away from Ianthe and clapped Adrian on the shoulder. "Today is the day. We've been preparing for this for a long time."

You have. But Adrian forced a smile and said, "Sure, Dad."

"There are plenty of contenders. The mermaid of your dreams is waiting in the crowd." His father shook his shoulder. "Choose carefully, Adrian."

Adrian swallowed past a lump in his throat. Ianthe put a light hand on his arm.

"Go on," she whispered encouragingly. "She's out there."

Adrian nodded at his mother and swam at his father's side toward the nearest young lady. Her tail was light pink, along with her hair. Her eyes were the colors of bubbles. Adrian figured inside her head, there wasn't much else. Next to her was a yellow-tailed girl, who gazed at Adrian suspiciously. She was probably a handmaid who was protective of her lady.

"Adrian, I'd like to introduce you to Lady

Jennifer, from the Caspian Sea," Poseidon said, gesturing to the pink-tailed mermaid.

Jennifer giggled. Adrian instantly found the sound annoying.

"You're so strong." Jennifer ran her fingers over Adrian's chest, and he had to fight not to recoil away. "I like that."

She was eyeing him like a piece of meat, already fitting her head for a crown. Adrian cleared his throat and said, "How do you do?"

Jennifer giggled again. "Very well, thank you."

"Jennifer's father has been Lord of the Caspian Sea for many centuries, son," Poseidon said. "Longer than almost anyone has held a title."

Like Adrian cared about titles. "Isn't the Caspian Sea enclosed?" he asked Jennifer curiously.

"Yes, the Caspian Sea is surrounded by land. We had to transform for a time until we could join the oceans again." Jennifer was barely paying attention to what Adrian was asking her. She was too focused on his biceps.

"So you go to the surface often," Adrian burst before he could control himself. Poseidon sent him a disapproving glance.

She shook her head. "Oh, no. I never go to the surface. You have to be a complete idiot to do so. I only go on land when we have to risk traveling somewhere… like for this."

She batted her eyelashes at him.

So she wasn't adventurous at all. Pass. His

father noticed the glazed-over look in Adrian's eyes and said, "Thank you, Lady Jennifer. We'll keep you in mind."

Jennifer was red-faced as Adrian swam away. She leaned in and whispered something vile to her yellow-tailed friend, who was shooting daggers at Adrian's back.

He was going to piss off a lot of women tonight. Happy Birthday to him.

"I thought we talked about this. You're not to bring it up," his father hissed at him in a low tone. "No talking about the surface!"

"Sorry." Adrian knew his father only let him get away with so much, because Poseidon felt the need to indulge him as long as he could, before the duties of the crown took over his life.

But… his father thought that Adrian only went up to the surface every now and then. If he truly knew how often… if he realized it was a daily thing… he'd never be allowed to leave the palace.

His father introduced him to mermaid after mermaid. Adrian kept waiting for that special moment, a powerful connection, some sort of love at first sight, but it never happened. None of the girls caught Adrian's eye or even held his attention.

It wasn't like he didn't like them as people… but as his queen? Most of the girls weren't concerned about him or his feelings, what he wanted, what he wished for and dreamed about. They just wanted that shell tiara on their head, and the big wedding that would come after.

They wanted to be *his queen*. They didn't want to be *his*.

These girls didn't know what they were getting into. It was a big job. The mermaid he chose would eventually become the Mistress of the Waves, Protector of the Depths. Poseidon might be King of the Sea, but it was Ianthe who kept it safe from the humans, his mother who restored the waters each year and tended to the care of each and every creature that dwelled within its reach.

Adrian knew he couldn't pick just *any* girl. His bride had to be kind... sweet... and had to hold great power without it going to her head.

He wouldn't find that in any of the girls here, that was for sure. Most of them were preening about, showing off the jewelry their parents had bought them or bragging on endlessly about bloodlines.

In Adrian's opinion, such things didn't matter. But... he had to remind himself that his queen wouldn't be the only one with a heavy burden. Someday, he'd be Lord of the Sea, and he'd have just as much responsibility on his shoulders as his father did.

The thought made him want to puke.

Ianthe noticed Adrian was less than enthusiastic about the whole affair. She pried him away from his father's side and wrapped an arm around him. "Feeling a little overwhelmed?"

The room was spinning. "There are so many."

And he had to pick one? The right one, *tonight*?

He wasn't even sure if he could remember half the names. How was he supposed to find his soulmate in this mess? The night would be over by the time introductions were finished.

"Give them a chance, Adrian," Ianthe said, quite gently. "I'm sure some of them are just as nervous as you are."

He wasn't sure about that. The girls who didn't get picked would go home and be free to marry whomever they chose. For him, there was no getting out of this.

Ianthe introduced him to another group of girls. The ones she chose were better than Poseidon's picks, but Adrian saw them immediately as friends, not lovers. As he spoke with these other girls, Adrian kept coming back to the girl on the boat, the one with the green eyes.

More like the one without fins, mind you, Adrian thought.

It was a pointless fantasy. He'd never see that particular girl ever again, and even if he did, he'd never be able to bring her back to Aquatica. She belonged on land. And him, in the sea.

But if she were here, and if she *were* a mermaid and not a human... he'd pick her in a minute. He knew it. There was just something about her that... clicked with him.

Hours passed, and the night lengthened. Adrian longed to sleep, but knew these kinds of parties could go on for days. After he'd met nearly a hundred girls, Adrian excused himself to get a bite to eat, but really, he wasn't hungry. He just needed an excuse to take a break. He sat at the table next to his father and picked at the swordfish that had been served.

His father was having a grand old time. You'd have thought it was his birthday and not his son's. Adrian leaned on the table and hoped he'd have a few more minutes of peace to be single before his parents shoved him out into the crowd again.

Then— the great doors blew open.

A giant wave pushed the doors apart, and merpeople quickly swam out of the way. There was a heavy sound, like a mass of water being shifted, and the entire room went dark for a moment before it brightened once again.

Merpeople started screaming. Adrian straightened up— finally, some excitement. An inky black cloud surrounded the water between the two doors, and from it emerged a figure Adrian hadn't seen in over ten years.

He was thin, with spines jetting out of his back and short black hair clipped into a point on his head. He had a goatee with a long face, and wore a smirk, like he knew everyone in the room was afraid of him. Eight tentacles, like those of squid, propelled him through the water toward the dining table. Like most mermen, he carried a weapon; a wooden staff made of driftwood, a shining black stone smoothed by the sea set at the top of it.

Stavros… the sea warlock.

His reputation preceded him. Stavros had a

talent for luring merpeople into traps with promises of whatever they wanted... for a price. The price was always, *always* more than what merpeople could afford to pay. Adrian didn't know how Stavros kept making deals, but Adrian supposed whoever did had to be desperate.

Thousands had fallen due to his dark magic. He'd even cursed an entire city of merpeople to dust and sand. Everyone was afraid of him— save for Poseidon, and Adrian.

Though for totally different reasons. Poseidon wasn't afraid, because he had more power than Stavros, and so, had no reason to be afraid of him. Adrian wasn't afraid of Stavros because he was stupid (as he would admit), and also because he truly believed that if it came down to a fight, he could handle him.

Although... Adrian had to admit... Stavros *was* intimidating. People swam out of the way as he moved through the room, creating a wide berth. It was clear that if Poseidon didn't have control of the sea, it would immediately belong to Stavros.

No one would dare challenge him.

"You are not welcome here," Poseidon said as Stavros approached the throne. "Speak what you must, and get out."

Stavros laughed low in his throat. His voice was deep, and alluring. Once could listen to him talk for hours and still be enchanted by the sound. "I merely came to wish my nephew a happy birthday."

"You haven't seen Adrian since he was an

infant," Poseidon growled. "Why would you come unless you wanted to ruin today, the most important of days?"

Stavros grinned his pointed teeth and stared at Adrian. "Why not let the boy decide?"

Stavros thought Adrian would make him a deal in order to find the perfect wife. No go. His uncle had made a very bad call, because if Adrian could, he'd stay single forever.

His father was expecting him to say something, so Adrian said, "You can stay. *If* you don't cause any trouble."

Merpeople gasped at the invitation. Even Stavros seemed momentarily shocked. But he shook it off quickly, and that arrogant smile was back. "Very well. I only ask for a moment of your time."

Adrian rose from the table. He knew his father's eyes were on him as he approached Stavros. The music, and the party, resumed, but the room was on edge, and wary.

"What do you want?" Adrian asked abruptly. He crossed his arms and stared at his uncle. "You wouldn't have come here if you didn't want something."

"You're like your father. So mistrustful. But I thank you for not throwing me out before I spoke with you," Stavros said. "It is important."

Stavros' appreciation sounded completely disingenuous. "So, you *do* want something."

"You should make a visit to my cave sometime." Stavros pounded his staff into the floor, and sparks flew through the water. "It'd be a special treat. I have a birthday present for you."

"I don't want anything from you."

"Nothing? Come, Adrian." Stavros made a *tsking* sound. "That's a lie, dear boy. There's *always* something merpeople desire that they can't have."

A picture of the girl from the boat broke into his mind, but Adrian quickly pushed it away. "So? Doesn't mean it's mine to take."

"Ah, boy. You're so much like your father." Stavros' stare was intense. "Or *are* you? I've heard the rumors, Adrian. You long to live on land. It calls to you. Can you imagine how much of an embarrassment you'd be to your father if your subjects found out you wish to exchange your tail for a pair of legs?"

"Stop it."

An image broke into his mind and took control over his vision; him, walking on land, enjoying the sun and taking in the feel of sand underneath his feet. He could see it, he could *feel it*…

But it was an illusion. Stavros was playing games with his head.

"I can make those dreams come true, Adrian. Anything you wish, and far more," Stavros offered.

"For a price. The answer is no." Adrian had run out of patience. His hands were bunched into fists. "Get out."

Stavros chuckled. "You will come, Adrian. We all want things that are out of our reach. You only need a push in the right direction."

His uncle shifted out of the party. Once his presence was gone, several merpeople breathed sighs of relief, and the jovial mood of the party returned.

Ianthe had been hovering at a close distance, protecting her son, willing to move in at a moment's notice. Now that Stavros was gone, she put her hands on Adrian's face. "Are you all right, my son?"

"Barely." Now he had to go back to picking brides and be reminded of his inescapable future — *again* — right after his uncle had taunted him with his wildest dreams. This was a special kind of torture.

"Take a swim. Return when you feel well." His mother patted him on the back, and Adrian hurried off. He avoided the mermaids who approached, slipping out of the grand hall and into one of the side parlors. He locked the door behind him with shaking fingers.

Adrian ran both hands though his hair and tried to take deep breaths. *I can't do this. I can't do this.*

He was sure he was becoming lightheaded.

"Hey!" Moona was outside, and Celer was floating nearby. She tapped on the window with her fin. "How's it going in there?"

Moona saw that Adrian was turning green and frowned. "Oh. Not well at all, I see."

"I'm freaking out, Moona." It was true. His heart was beating so fast he swore it would burst out of his chest and swim away.

"There's no need for all that," Moona said. "Come on. Let's ditch."

Adrian yanked at his hair. He *wanted* to, but… this birthday meant more than all the others, especially to his father. But would it really be so bad to skip out on his own party?

Adrian opened the doors and peeked around the corner. He could hear his father laughing boisterously with a group of mermen that he swore were part whale.

His father wasn't even paying attention. He wouldn't know that he was gone. Adrian had seven days after the party to pick a queen. He could put it off… just one more night.

"Okay. I'm coming, before they start looking for me." Adrian swam round the back, and squeezed through a tiny window in the kitchen he'd been slipping out of since he knew how to swim. He met Moona outside, and she pressed herself against him when they joined again.

"Where do you want to go?" she asked.

Adrian shimmied out of the stuffy shirt and threw it aside. "Any- where but here. Celer, let's get out of here. Celer?"

Moona and Adrian turned. Celer had his head pressed up against the window, small bubbles flitting out of his nostrils as he looked inside with wide eyes at the pretty mermaids.

"Babes…" Celer said in a delusion, staring through the window with an open mouth.

"Oh, forget him." Adrian waved a hand at his seahorse. "Let's just go."

Celer didn't even notice them leave. Adrian was sure if they switched places, Celer would have no problem choosing a mate— only issue he'd have is picking *which one.*

Adrian swam away from the palace as quickly as he could. He wished he could be anywhere else, be *anyone* else... even if it was just for a moment.

The truth was, the offer Stavros had given him was tempting. Too tempting. Adrian had almost said yes.

And though he'd never admit it to himself, he was still considering it.

CHAPTER FOUR

ISA

The salty breeze Isa inhaled through her nose was like the original breath of life.

Isa held her surfboard tightly to her side and tried not to dance. She loved the feeling of the waves crashing against her bare feet, and the way she sank into the sand as the ocean rolled over her. A full moon lit the sea in a white halo, a perfect glow under the starry sky.

She'd been out here for hours, waiting for Harbor and Shelly to get done with clubbing until the wee hours of the night. It was close to dawn, she knew. She was tired, but she didn't long for her bed. She wanted the ocean. She enjoyed being out here and watching the waves roll in... enjoyed being alone. The water was the only thing that understood her.

She wished she didn't have to live a life on land.

More than anything, she wanted to be a part of the sea.

The storm was still approaching. It had been raining off and on, so Isa had been waiting to make her move and start surfing. She couldn't wait much longer, however. She needed to be out there, storm or no storm.

"Hey, Isa!" There was a shout over the waves. Isa smiled when she saw her friends approaching, boards tucked underneath their arms.

Harbor and Shelly were Isa's best friends because... well... they weren't from Coral Bay. They were college students at the university, like she was.

"What up, bitch," Harbor said. She gave Isa a high-five when she joined her side. "How are the waves?"

"Just about perfect." Isa fastened the surfboard to her ankle with the Velcro clasp, ignoring the approaching storm on the horizon. "You guys ready for this?"

Shelly shivered. "It's a bit cold, isn't it? Shouldn't we go home?"

"The water's fine, Shelly. You're such a wuss," Harbor complained.

Isa didn't care if the water was cold. She wanted to ride some waves. "You girls can stay on shore if you want. I won't be long. I just wanted to head out for a bit."

"Breakfast would be better." Shelly was shivering. *"The Flying Seagull* has the best brunch, and boys."

Shelly wasn't interested in going anywhere unless there were boys involved. But Isa needed more than a quick hookup. She wanted to feel alive. She needed something *real*. "It's still dark. We'll go there in a bit. Just a quick ride, I promise."

Isa had no intention of going to *The Flying Seagull*, but she said it anyway, just to make Shelly happy.

At the mention of boys and brunch, however, Harbor's attention was captured. "Shelly's right. We've been surfing a lot lately. We should do something different for a change. It's already starting to rain again."

Isa's only way of handling life was to surf, but she didn't want to tell her friends that. She went surfing even more than they thought. If they knew how much she was on her board, they'd think she had a serious problem.

A large lightning bolt lit up the ocean behind her. Shelly and Harbor took a few steps back, but Isa wasn't afraid. If anything, she was more excited.

The wind started to pick up. The rain was starting to fall heavily now, and dark clouds were gathering, blocking out the moon and stars. Isa hadn't seen a storm whip up so suddenly and so violently since the last hurricane had blown through. The waves were increasing in size and intensity. Only the most experienced surfers could expect to head into the ocean and survive.

But if you could ride those waves… man, what a thrill you'd get from it. It'd be more than worth it.

Isa was in the mood to tempt fate tonight.

"Isa, no. I know what you're thinking," Shelly said the minute she saw the fire ignite in Isa's eyes. She tried to grab her, but Isa slid out of the way.

"I'm only going out for a sec!" Isa shouted. She ran into the water before her friends could stop her, and was on her board just as lightning lit up the sky.

"Crazy bitch!" she heard Harbor call over the storm. Isa crouched down on her board, and it was then she started flying.

There was nothing better than the feel of a board underneath her as she skimmed over water. Nothing. It was like drawing energy directly from the ocean and injecting it into Isa's veins. She laughed with ecstasy as she expertly weaved her board against the water. For a brief moment, Isa thought that she could control the sea herself.

In the distance, a monster wave was growing. She spotted it in the corner of her eye as it rapidly approached, the size of a small building. The sea was growing stronger now, agitated by the demands of the storm and Isa's arrogant claim to it.

Her first thought was to turn back and head toward the shore. Isa knew better than to take her chances. No one she knew had ever conquered a wave that big.

She'd be the first.

Isa heard the shouts of Harbor and Shelly,

telling her not to do it. Isa would show them. She smiled and gave a happy cry as the tip of her board broke upon the monster wave.

She struggled to maintain her balance the moment her board was upon the wave. It was stronger than she thought, something she'd under-estimated.

But she could do this— she could handle it. Hell, it was the only thing in her life she *could* handle. Slowly, she gained control, water droplets spraying off the wave and sticking to her face. She felt the powerful rumble of the wave underneath her feet as the board shook, and the roar that it made in her ears as it crashed around her.

Isa felt joy explode in her chest as she spotted the end of the wave. She'd done it! She'd mastered surfing! Shelly and Harbor were cheering from the shore, and Isa's smile grew wider at the thought of their reaction once she returned to the beach.

Then something distracted her... the sight of that green fin again, and a boy's face.

That broken second of concentration was all it took. Isa lost control. The violent wave tossed her into the sky, and her board broke. The line tying her to the surfboard snapped, and Isa felt her nose and mouth fill with seawater as she tumbled head-first into the ocean, dragged down by the sheer power of the sea.

She thought she could hear Shelly and Harbor's screams as she went under.

The entire world went dark, and Isa's eyes

burned as she opened them within the saltiness. She tried to swim, but in the darkness and swirling tumult, she couldn't be sure which way was up, and she wasn't strong enough to resist the pull of the undertow. The wave churned her over and over, and Isa found herself swirling within the depths without a way out.

This was it. She'd finally gotten her wish. She was going to be a part of the sea, forever.

She was going to die.

CHAPTER FIVE

ADRIAN

A drian and Moona were listlessly swimming around, not quite sure where they were going, but figuring they were going somewhere important.

Adrian could feel it in his bones. Wherever he and Moona were headed, it was of the utmost importance. He didn't know why, but he'd told Moona so.

"This feels right," he said. "Like… we're *supposed* to be out here, and not at my party."

"You and your superstitions," Moona grumbled, but she let Adrian be consumed by his fantasies. It was too much work to talk him out of his fanciful daydreams.

Adrian had been nothing but worried after they'd left the palace. He worried about how his father would react to his absence, how his guests would take it, and mostly, what his mother would say.

But his worries got farther and farther away the closer he got to the shoreline. It was like, for him, approaching land was the only way to calm his frantic heart.

There was a storm whipping up. It was a nasty one. There was thunder and lightning in the sky, and the waves were so strong they tossed Adrian and Moona back and forth between them.

Adrian knew the storm was caused by his father. Poseidon had finally noticed his absence. Adrian could hear what his father would say once he returned. *Irresponsible! We've been planning this party for years, and you run off in the most disrespectful way possible! How can I possibly believe you'll ever be ready to be king?*

The shouts in his ears dulled as he got closer and closer to the beach. *Just a little farther,* Adrian told himself.

"I don't like this, Adrian," Moona called over the storm's rampage. "It's getting hard for me to keep up with you!"

"Just float for a bit, Moona," Adrian told her. "I'll be okay on my own."

He left Moona behind as he continued on his quest. The water grew shallow— shallower than he was used to. Adrian paused for a moment to survey his surroundings. If he had to go back so soon, he was at least going to enjoy the few precious seconds he had...

Someone was on the water. Adrian was familiar with surfing, but he'd never tried it himself, and never in a storm. The human who was surfing now was either crazy, or they had a death wish.

Adrian spotted a mass of blonde hair, and his curiosity peaked. He swam closer, against the roar of the waves. He thought he was seeing things for a moment, but on closer inspection, he found that his eyes hadn't deceived him.

It was the girl! The same one whom he'd spotted on the boat earlier! Adrian couldn't believe his luck. What was she doing out here, tempting the favor of the gods? Poseidon had claimed many souls who'd dared to question him on the water, and he wouldn't mind claiming one more.

Adrian decided he couldn't let that happen. He'd protect her from his father's wrath. Adrian swam after the girl, keeping himself submerged underwater so she wouldn't see him. He wasn't sure what he was doing, but he figured his presence would be enough to ensure her safety during his father's tantrum.

Adrian became enchanted by the sight of the girl's lips, her soft eyelids, and her excited expression as she soared over him like an angel on the surfboard. They moved as one, him beneath the waves and her above them, and for a moment, Adrian felt a strong connection pass between them that went deeper than anything he'd ever experienced.

Then Adrian made a major mistake. He got too

close, and his tail poked out of the water. He turned over, and his face caught the girl's eyes. She looked down, and her expression widened in shock. With that vital moment, she tumbled into the sea.

Adrian panicked. He watched as the girl was tossed around underwater like a doll, helpless against the sea's power. He knew he had a decision to make.

If he saved her, the secret of the mermaids would be discovered.

And if he didn't... she'd surely drown.

Adrian wasn't going to let that happen, not for any secret. So he dove in after the girl even as Moona was screaming at him to be careful.

He had trouble maneuvering around the waves — his father must be *enraged*. But he was the son of Poseidon, and he had some power, too. Adrian commanded the waves to calm around him, his magic fighting his father's. The seas obeyed him, quieting so there was a soft patch of calm amongst the raging ocean.

The girl's body stopped spinning in the water, but she'd gone limp. She'd passed out.

He had to get her onto land and get some air into her lungs, fast. It was her only chance. Adrian wrapped his arms around the girl. He was surprised at how light and perfect she felt against his chest, two lost pieces fitting together. It was like her body was made for Adrian... or maybe, Adrian for her.

It was easy for him to carry her through the water... the easiest thing he ever did. His magic ensured the water stayed calm around him as he lifted the girl so her head was bobbing out of the water. He headed to a secret place... his cove.

There was a small beach tucked away near a cove that had long been forgotten. Adrian had claimed it long ago, and used it whenever he got the chance to come on land.

Adrian always got excited when he went on shore, but his excitement was currently quashed by worry. He placed the girl on the beach and scooted onto the beach.

"Come on," Adrian muttered when her chest didn't move. He began pumping her heart, doing thirty reps before breathing deeply into her mouth, filling her lungs with needed air.

She didn't move. Adrian continued, begging her now.

"Please, *please* wake up," Adrian pleaded, like his own life depended on it. "Don't leave me now."

He wasn't so sure why he'd grown so attached to this person he didn't even know. All he knew was if he lost her now, he was pretty sure he'd lose himself, too.

Finally, water sputtered up from her mouth. The girl coughed, spitting up what was in her lungs before she passed out again.

"Oh, Adrian." Moona was swimming back and forth anxiously along the shore. "This is bad. This is very bad."

"She's breathing," Adrian whispered, enchanted by her appearance. "Isn't it a miracle?"

"Just leave her there," Moona said. "She'll be all right."

Adrian wasn't so sure. "I've got to make sure she's okay."

"Her friends will find her. They're looking for her," Moona insisted.

That wasn't good enough. His tail flopped in the sand. *He* wanted to be the one to save her, not her friends. He didn't want to leave her side, not when she was like this.

"Wait for me back at the palace, Moona," he told her. "I'll be there soon."

"What am I supposed to tell your father?" she hissed. "That is, if he doesn't chop me up for fish food first!"

"You'll make something up." Adrian pulled himself farther onto the beach, and Moona let out an unhappy sound. She dove back into the sea and swam away, listening to Adrian's command.

When Adrian was on his back and lying beside the girl, he closed his eyes and willed his powers to work. As he used his magic, his tail split and knit itself into two legs. Adrian stood shakily, and stumbled a few times trying to catch his balance.

One thing about being on shore— he wasn't good at walking. He was sure he looked like a drunken idiot. The magic wouldn't work for very long. In less than two hours, the pain would be unbearable, and he'd lose the ability to breathe out of water. He'd have to return to the sea eventually.

But two hours would be enough to get the girl to safety.

Adrian headed into the cove to find some jeans he had hid in a crag behind a large rock. He put them on, then headed back to the beach. Dawn was starting to rise now. Adrian knelt in the sand, to take the girl in his arms and carry her to safety.

But as Adrian stooped downward, something happened that he didn't expect.

The girl's eyes opened... and they latched onto Adrian's for the second time.

There was no going back now. The strong connection that formed in that moment, Adrian knew, was permanent.

He'd found his queen. But she was the one person that Adrian could never, ever have.

CHAPTER SIX

ISA

There was a boy with a glowing halo above her.

He was beautiful. He had red hair cropped short around his head, which was glistening wet with droplets from the sea. His skin was pale, like the foam that rose over the waves, and he had blue eyes that reflected the water.

Isa thought he was the most gorgeous person she'd ever seen. It didn't help that he was half-naked. God, those abs. They looked like they'd been chiseled by the heavens.

"Hey," he said softly, and the sound of his voice was like the wave she'd rode— gentle, yet powerful at the same time. "You're awake. I was worried you wouldn't make it."

Her head was pounding. Just how much salt water had she swallowed? "I…"

"Easy," he said as she tried to get up, and then

fell backwards. He caught her before her back hit the sand. "You took a bad tumble through the water. If I hadn't saved you—"

"Saved me?" The words came out slurred through her lips. This was impossible. No one, and Isa knew, *no one*, could swim through the storm that had nearly drowned her. An Olympic athlete would've been swallowed up like they were a guppy. She didn't care how good a swimmer this guy was, there was no way he was the one who'd rescued her.

But Isa knew... she had to have been rescued. There was no way she'd just washed up on the beach. Not with the way those waves were. She should be floating in the middle of the ocean, and yet, here she was, safe on land.

The guy grimaced, like he'd said too much. "Never mind. We need to get you to a hospital."

"I'm..." Isa's weak protests were muted when she felt a harsh wave of nausea press in on her, and her stomach rolled. She'd never taken this bad of a fall before. Her entire body was numb. Something could be broken, and she wouldn't even know it.

Isa could feel the waves slowly wash over her as they swelled in and out. As the breeze passed her by, she caught the scent of her savior. Salt water and sunlight, with a bit of pineapple. Though her lungs were filled with saltwater before, they were working fine now.

She took a deep inhale and reveled in the guy's sweet scent. It was just perfect. Talk about an aphrodisiac. Smelling him made Isa go crazy for him, though she was half out of it and didn't even know his name.

"Can you stand?" he asked.

Isa tried getting up again, but her head lolled and he said, "Not a good idea. I'll carry you."

He kneeled down and slipped an arm beneath her knees and shoulders, then rose in one fluid movement. Isa felt like she weighed no more than a feather as her body drifted through the air, supported by strong arms.

"What's your name?" she mumbled, before she bubbled out of consciousness again.

The stranger paused for a moment, before he said, "Adrian."

Isa passed out then, just as Adrian was carrying her up the beach and away from the water.

SHE WOKE UP TO THE SOUND OF MACHINES beeping a short time later. There was an IV in her arm, and her stomach felt worse than ever. There were large bruises she hadn't noticed before that covered her arms, and it hurt to move. *That wave really kicked my ass.*

Adrian was sitting in a chair across from her on the right side of the bed. He gave her a reassuring smile, and she felt her insides wiggle.

Not a great way to kick off a first date with a cute guy. Wait... what?

"Good news. You're going to be fine," Adrian said— like Isa cared. "They pumped out the rest of the salt water. You're dehydrated, but mostly okay. You should be able to go home soon."

She coughed. "That's good, I guess. I hate to ask, but do you mind giving me a ride home?" Isa didn't know why she trusted this random stranger, but she did... naturally. He'd saved her life. He wouldn't hurt her.

"I don't have a car. I just carried you here."

"You carried me all the way from the beach to *here*?" What did this guy lift when he was working out, buildings? Who could be that strong to carry someone for miles?

"It wasn't that far. Besides, I don't need a car."

"Who doesn't need a car in Coral Bay?" she wondered aloud. It was a small town, and everything was far apart.

"I get around in a different way." He smiled again.

Isa was struck by a sudden thought. "My long-board. I left it at the beach." *Shit.* She ran a hand through her hair, certain it was gone now. Her surf-board was demolished too, all in one night.

"I've got it, along with your stuff." Adrian held it up, and nudged her backpack with his foot. "I went back and fetched it before you woke up."

Relief ran through her. Apparently, Adrian ran marathons, too. "Seriously, thank you. Do you go the university? I haven't seen you around before."

"No. I'm not a college student." He laughed, as if the idea was funny.

"Well… do you live around here?" she pressed, hoping it was a yes.

"Eh…" he rubbed the back of his neck. "Not really."

So not a local, then… but definitely not a snowbird. Maybe he was from a different part of Florida.

"What were you doing out on the beach? I thought me and my friends were the only ones out there," she said.

"Just visiting. I was swimming."

Swimming, last night? In *that* mess? He was crazier than she was.

She liked it.

Isa was so caught up in Adrian's eyes she hadn't noticed that he'd gone quiet. His skin had changed color, taking on a slight grey tinge. Adrian almost looked… sick.

"Are you okay?" she asked.

"Yeah." He made a pained face, and stood up. "I'm sorry. I have to go."

This stranger probably had his own life. But on the inside, Isa wanted to beg him to stay.

"I would stay, if I could." Adrian reached down. He took her hand delicately in his and gave it a squeeze, then bent down and brushed his lips over top of it, giving her a kiss.

The movement sent shivers down her spine, and the feel of his lips against her skin made her entire body go on fire. That one little gesture made Isa want to rip her clothes off and jump him.

Adrian gently put her hand back onto the mattress. "See you around." He turned on his heel. His legs wobbled as he walked out of the room, like an infant learning to walk. Swimming in the storm must've really taken it out of him.

He needs to see a doctor more than I do, Isa thought. She mused on the kiss. It seemed like something a prince would do. But that was stupid.

Isa rummaged through her backpack to find her phone. She texted Harbor and Shelly to let them know where she was. Fifteen minutes later, her girl-friends stormed in like they were charging the gates of hell. They berated Isa for not calling them sooner.

"We thought you'd *died,*" Shelly wept.

"I don't understand how you could do this to us. We *told* you not to go out there!" Harbor shouted. "And we missed brunch. You're such a bitch."

Harbor's favorite word was bitch. Not that Isa didn't deserve it. She'd driven her friends mad with worry after she'd sunk under that wave.

"I'm sorry you guys didn't hear from me. I was busy dealing with Adrian," Isa said.

"Adrian?" Shelly's eyes widened.

"Yeah. He was a guy who pulled me out of the water," she said. "He carried me to the hospital."

"Oooh," Shelly wagged her eyebrows. "Like Hercules."

"Oh, okay, false alarm, Shelly," Harbor said

sarcastically, her hands on her hips. "It's *fine* we thought Isa was dead, because she was playing damsel-in-distress in order to get some dick."

"If you had seen how hot this dude was, you would understand," Isa joked.

But Shelly took her seriously. She pulled up a chair to the bedside and leaned forward. "Tell us every detail."

Isa confessed to her friends the conversation with Adrian, and how he'd kissed her hand.

"Have you heard of him before?" Isa asked hopefully.

"Us? No, we don't know him, and we know everybody in this town." Harbor looked to Shelly, and she shook her head. "Are you sure this guy is real?"

"Positive. I'm not making it up," Isa said.

Her friends were looking at her like she had swallowed too much seawater — like she was crazy.

Maybe she was. What if Adrian was just a product of her imagination? But then, how had she gotten to the hospital?

Harbor drove her back home. Her pushy friend insisted on staying, but Isa was able to chase her out after she said for the thousandth time she was going to bed.

"My dad is seriously gonna kill me," she muttered as she walked in the door. She opened it slowly, waiting for the impending implosion.

But it was silent. Only Paola was there, sweeping the floor and humming along to Selena.

"Oh, hello, *chica*," Paola said casually. "Are you hungry? I'm making lunch."

Paola didn't know she'd been in the hospital, because she'd never been informed. Her father hasn't realized she'd snuck out, nor had he noticed her absence that morning. He hadn't even realized she'd been gone.

It hit her hard that if Adrian hadn't come by when he did, she could've been missing for *days*, and her father would've never started looking.

Isa shook the tears out of her eyes. "No, Paola. I'm not hungry."

She darted past the bewildered maid and to her room. Isa slammed the door shut and jumped on the bed, falling on her back to gaze up at the ceiling.

Her room was various shades of blue. Scattered all around it was her mermaid collection... there were mermaid plastic dolls, mermaid pillows, posters and paintings of mermaids, stuffed mermaids, even a mermaid bedspread. The current explosion of mermaid items at the mall had done nothing to curb her obsession. She was seriously running out of room to put it all.

She hadn't changed the design of her room since she was twelve. When she was little, she dreamed of being in the ocean, of having a tail and swimming far away.

Maybe, if she was a beautiful mermaid, her mother would've stayed.

It seemed stupid now.

Isa turned on her back and stared up at the ceiling. She tried not to think of her father. Instead, she thought about Adrian.

He wasn't real. Like her fake, plastic mermaids, he was a figment of her imagination.

This was her reality. And as much as she wanted it to be a fairy tale, it wasn't, and it sucked.

Isa closed her eyes and wished things were different.

CHAPTER SEVEN

ADRIAN

"Come on, Moona. It's just one day. Please, for me."

Adrian was in his room at the palace, trying to convince a *very* stubborn Moona to create a distraction so he could slip away. He'd spent most of the day yesterday putzing around, swimming from here to there without any sort of destination, before he'd snuck back into the palace late at night when no one was looking.

He knew the moment his father realized he was back in the castle he'd get yelled at for ditching the party, and harassed about picking out a mermaid for his upcoming wedding. Adrian was in *no way* ready to deal with that.

His heart had already chosen for him. And it didn't matter if it was the worst choice ever made in history… Adrian was going to find a way to make it work.

Now all the guards were looking for him, and Adrian knew if he didn't get out of the palace fast, he'd be dragged right back to his father. He had to find a way to escape.

That's where Moona came in. Poseidon was opposed to sea creatures being in the castle, but he'd made an exception for Moona, because Adrian was her best friend. If she swam throughout the palace, merpeople would chase after her demanding to know where Adrian had gone.

And then Adrian would slip right out again. But there was one problem; Moona wasn't willing to go along with it.

"You must think I'm insane," Moona said. "I'm tired of covering up for you, Adrian!"

This had happened one too many times, and Adrian had never been in this much trouble before. Moona was giving him a hard no.

"I'll do anything, Moona, I promise," he begged. "Just do me this favor. I have to see her."

Leaving Isa in the hospital yesterday had been something that'd nearly killed him. He knew he should be by her side taking care of her, not in the middle of the ocean arguing with a stubborn manatee.

It was madness. The sea called to him, but his mate did, too. Both were undeniable urges that he couldn't satisfy at the same time. If he was with one, he wasn't with the other.

Adrian wondered if he'd be cursed to suffer like

this forever. He was undeniably in love with both of them, he knew that.

But he knew the sea. He didn't know Isa. That was something he wanted to rectify, if just a little, before he informed his father of his decision.

His mind was already made up. How Poseidon would take it, Adrian was sure wouldn't be well.

"They're going to know I'm *lying*, Adrian. They'll be confused when they see we're not together." Moona swayed back and forth in the water. "I said no."

Adrian shrugged. "Okay. Fine. I'm leaving with or without your help."

"Adrian, *wait*," Moona hissed, and she planted herself in front of him. "Are you sure about this? Is she worth the risk?"

He stared coldly at her. "She's the one, Moona. I wouldn't tell you that unless I was sure."

Adrian swam underneath her and came up at the window. He pried it open and slipped out.

At the last minute, Moona gave a heavy sigh, hung her head, and swam out the bedroom door. Merpeople immediately started following her, calling her name.

Adrian smiled. "Thanks, Moona."

Adrian swam toward the surface, where he knew no other merfolk dared to linger. From there he kept up a steady pace, until he reached his private cove and pulled himself out of the water and onto the beach.

Out of his net bag he pulled a slim glass bottle,

filled with glowing liquid. He'd stolen it from a merfolk apothecary long ago and had been saving it for something like this. Adrian was glad he'd been smart enough to keep it, and not use it foolishly.

A transfiguration potion. Little magic. Not very powerful. But it would enable him to walk on land for a full day rather than just a few hours. Adrian was sure this was all he would need to find Isa.

He had to be careful. Once he drank this potion, it would become like poison to him. He couldn't drink it again — not for at least another month.

Adrian had to make this day count.

He popped off the cork and tilted the potion back into his mouth, ignoring his gag reflex and forcing himself to swallow. A pain rolled in his gut, and he grimaced as his fin turned into two legs.

Wobbling worse than yesterday, Adrian retrieved his pants from the hidden nook in the cove, along with a shirt and sandals he'd found on a nearby yacht. He put them on and started walking around to find Isa.

Adrian followed his instincts. He knew they would lead him to Isa, wherever she was.

She wasn't in Coral Bay. That much he could feel. She was outside of town — not too far away, but not too close. Adrian got on a bus and rode it until he could feel the pull inside of him screaming to get off.

He disembarked in a large city, a touristy area with shops and towns. Adrian kept his head down and ignored the giggles of the beautiful girls that passed him by as he entered a college campus. He was only looking for one woman.

He was nervous. Adrian had never been this far from the sea before. Even now, there was a burning feeling in his chest that made it uncomfortable to be so distant from the water.

But the burning wasn't the worst problem. If he couldn't get back in time before the potion wore off, he would die. Mermaids couldn't last long out of water, not without extensive magic. Eventually he'd turn back into a merman, and his lungs would no longer breathe the oxygen in the air without water to filtrate it.

The risk of death would be worth it, to find Isa.

Adrian wandered around campus until his gut led him to an aquarium on a lake near the food courts. He entered the aquarium and paid for a ticket, looking around at the various sea folk contained in glass tanks.

Adrian always thought it was funny humans sought to keep fish in tanks, but hey, they were humans. There wasn't much use in trying to explain anything they did. The fish followed him as he ventured through the aquarium. They knew who he was and whispered to him to let them out.

Adrian felt sorry for them, but at the same time, knew there wasn't much he could do. He could release these fish, but the humans would find others to take their place— not to mention he'd blow his cover.

Finally, he found her. There she was, sitting on

the edge of a fountain, bent over a textbook. Her hair was pulled back, there were square glasses on her face, and she was frantically scribbling something into a notebook. She was wearing an orange shirt with a dolphin insignia— the aquarium's logo — with jeans and white tennis shoes that were impeccably clean.

"I didn't know you worked here," Adrian said. Isa's head snapped up. She was so surprised she reeled backward, and her eyes widened as she careened toward the fountain.

Adrian caught her just before she hit the water. He held her body close... he could hear her frantic breathing, and the quick beating of her heart against his firm chest.

This was everything he ever wanted.

"Uh, hey." Isa parted a strand of hair behind her ear, still wrapped within his arms. She blushed pink, and Adrian thought it was unbearably cute. "How'd you find me?"

"I was just visiting the aquarium," Adrian lied. He brought her up to a standing position and put her on two feet. Only then did he let her go.

He gestured to the notebook. "Working on homework?"

"Just got off my shift," she said. "I was finishing up an essay I had that's due tomorrow for biology class." She blushed again and looked down.

What was it about her that was so irresistible? He wasn't sure, but he wanted to drag her back to the sea again… show her who he *truly* was, not this two-legged mask he was forced to wear.

"I've been thinking about you," Adrian confessed. Talking to her was so easy. They'd just met— barely talked— but it was like he'd known her forever.

"Yeah. I'm still recovering, but the doctor said by tomorrow I'll be back to normal," she said. "Thanks again, for saving my life."

He shrugged and gave her a smile. "No thanks needed."

He picked up the book and rifled through it. "Biology, huh? You left out that it was about sea life."

"I want to be a marine biologist," she said. "Sorry if it's nerdy."

She truly did sound sorry. Why? Adrian thought it was cool. She already had a love for the ocean, and for the animals that lived there. She couldn't have picked a more perfect career. "I don't think it's nerdy. And if it is, so what? You've got to be really smart to be a marine biologist. That's pretty badass."

She sighed. "Some people think it's stupid."

"People in general are stupid, Izzy." He laughed. "Everyone has an opinion, but I've found the only one that matters is your own."

Her head tilted and she said, "You're pretty confident. I bet you have an amazing job."

Adrian hesitated. What was he supposed to tell

her? "I, uh… mostly help my dad," he said. "Family business."

Wasn't a lie, exactly. But the truth was so much more.

"My family has one of those, too. A dolphin tour boat," Isa supplemented.

She assumed his family owned a tourist joint. It was reasonable to consider. Most locals down here did.

Adrian hated lying to his mate, but he figured he'd tell her the truth eventually, so he said, "It's something like that."

He changed the subject. "So… you still haven't told me what's so bad about being a marine biologist. What do people *expect* you to be?"

"I don't know." She stared downward. "My dad's in the military. I think everyone expected I was going to marry some powerful Navy official. Stay inside. Be kept."

Adrian felt a wave of rage rise and fall within his chest. How *dare* anyone think of imprisoning Isa like that! She deserved to be free. Yes, Adrian knew that he would someday be king of the sea, and if Isa agreed, she would be his queen.

But beside him, Isa would have equal power… and even power that went beyond his own. She wouldn't be locked up and *kept* as a pretty pet for him to have on his arm.

"That's so dumb." Adrian sat beside her. "You totally made the right decision, to pursue an education."

Isa gnawed on her lower lip. "I don't know. My dad doesn't agree. He only pays for my tuition because he thinks I'll meet some rich guy at college, and once I do, I'll drop out."

"How silly." He couldn't imagine Isa being with anyone but him. He nudged her. "Come on. You seem hungry. What do you say we go out for a late lunch?"

Her eyes brightened, but she hesitated. "I don't know. I have a lot of work to get done."

"You can do it later. Have a bit of fun."

At his prodding, Isa gave in. "All right." She put the book back in her backpack and slung it over her shoulder as she stood. "Where to?"

"I know this awesome seafood place. You're going to love it," he said.

They wandered through the aquarium to get to the back exit. As they passed through the various exhibits, Adrian pointed out fish after fish, naming them all and explaining to Isa all the little things he knew about them. He was sure she had an idea of what they were, as she was studying to be a marine biologist, but there were some things about the sea not even the most experienced human knew. He couldn't help it. He wanted to impress her, and it was obvious she was into marine life.

"You sure know a lot about fish," Isa said. Her tone was riddled with a hint of suspicion, but what could she guess? The reality was something she couldn't imagine, not even in her wildest dreams.

"I grew up in the sea. It's all I know," he answered cryptically.

Isa stared straight ahead and didn't answer. They entered into the sunlight, and Adrian cringed as it hit his skin— he didn't like feeling so dried out... so hot. It was uncomfortable. But he would put up with it for her.

They wandered to Isa's car, which was light blue in color. They drove out of the university, and back toward the ocean, while Adrian gave directions. The closer they got to water, the more relieved Adrian felt.

Adrian noticed she listened to K-Pop. Isa was quiet... it was like she didn't even realize it was on.

"So you like K-Pop," Adrian asked, just as a way to make conversation. He'd hardly heard it before, but some of the mermaids who lived in the bodies of water around the Korean peninsula were obsessed with it.

"Oh, yeah, sorry." She fumbled to change it. "I'll put on something else."

"Don't." He grabbed her hand. "I don't mind."

When they touched, Adrian had the feeling of being knocked over by a powerful wave— it sent him inwardly reeling backward.

Isa could feel it too, he could tell... by the astonished look in her eyes, she'd experienced the powerful feeling that had ricocheted up both of their arms.

Their mating bond was only getting stronger. Adrian was ready for it, but Isa wasn't.

"Pull off here," Adrian pointed, and Isa did as she was told. When they got out of her car, she avoided his eyes.

On the beach was a tiny yellow shack with a gray shuttered roof, surrounded by picnic tables shadowed by blue umbrellas. The shack was barely held together, and had hardly survived the last hurricane, but Adrian was glad it still stood. For all his hatred of humans, this was the only place Poseidon would come on land for. He'd often brought Adrian here as a small child... but they hadn't been here together since Adrian was around ten. Overfishing was getting bad and the pollution worse, so Poseidon had ruled that no one was to venture to the surface. Adrian had broken his rule and come here many times alone, though he often wished his father still accompanied him.

It was quite busy, even after lunch. They stood in line, Isa hiding behind her orange, plastic sunglasses.

"I've never been here before, and I've lived here all my life," Isa said quizzically.

"It's Coral Bay's best secret," Adrian said. "Watch. You'll see."

When they got up to the window, Adrian ordered them two dinners. The food came out in round baskets, nestled in that day's newspaper. It contained a pound of crab, steaming and red, with a large cup of butter and tongs for snapping. The sides included homemade coleslaw, a hunk of corn-bread and collard greens.

Two root beers were placed on the table. "Nothing like drinking a cold one on the beach during a nice day," Adrian said, and he popped the cap. As he took a swig, he saw Isa crack open a crab leg. She devoured the juicy middle, and her face melted.

"Wow" she mumbled. "This is so good."

"Told you it was incredible." Adrian started in on his own meal, and they ate while watching the waves roll in. Two little kids played by the beach, and their parents closely watched as laughter from the surrounding tables matched the sound of the ocean. There wasn't a cloud in the sky. It was truly a perfect day.

"Enjoying yourself?" Adrian asked happily. It'd only been minutes, but Isa had devoured most of her meal already.

"Yes." Isa struggled to talk around a full mouth before swallowing. "This is incredible. I've never had anything like this. At least... not in a long time."

"What do you mean?" Adrian took a bite of cornbread and raised an eyebrow.

"Me and my dad used to come to tiny seaside shacks like this. Our favorite place to eat was on the beach."

She gave a tiny sigh. "That doesn't happen anymore."

"Sorry." He frowned. "My dad and I used to do this a lot, too. But I guess he's too busy now."

"Parents get too busy for their kids once they stop being cute." Isa shrugged. "It happens."

"You obviously like crab," Adrian suggested.

"I enjoy eating seafood. It's my favorite. But lately, all my dad brings home is fast food." She looked down at her basket. "I shouldn't complain. But it's getting really old."

The conversation had turned too sobering, so Adrian picked up their finished baskets and threw them away.

"Come on," he said, and he extended a hand to her. "Let's go for a walk."

Isa gave his hand a wary stare before slowly slipping her own into it. "Okay."

Adrian had only meant to pull her up from her seat, but before he knew what was happening, they were holding hands. Isa didn't pull away, just kept her hand in his as they strolled along the shoreline.

Adrian wanted this to be *more* than magic. He wanted Isa to like him for him, not because the mating bond forced her to. It took all his will to pull his arm away, but he did.

"So," he started. "Been surfing since that night?"

Isa laughed. "No. My friends would kill me if I tried. But I've been saving up money to get a new board. I want to get back out on the waves as soon as possible."

"That fall didn't scare you?"

"Not at all." Her eyes were flashing. "I'm addicted

to surfing. Can't get enough. I've won a lot of trophies. Not to brag or anything, but I've been on a board since before I could walk. My dad taught me."

"Your dad sounds pretty cool."

"He... *was* pretty cool." Isa trailed off. "Then he got obsessed with his job."

"What does he do?"

"He's in the Navy." Isa bent down to pick up a shell. "But all that means is he never tells me anything."

Isa brushed off the shell. She stared at it in her cupped hands, and Adrian thought how pretty it would look in her hair.

Isa chucked the shell back into the sea. "School and studying are my life right now. That, along with working at the aquarium, and on my uncle's tour boat, keeps me busy. What about you?"

"I have a lot of free time. I like exploring. I collect things, usually stuff people don't want. My friend Moona calls it junk." He laughed.

"Where do you collect it from? Antique stores?"

"Naw." He shook his head. "Shipwrecks, mostly."

"That's so unique. I haven't been diving in a while." Isa sighed. "I've been meaning to get back into it."

"Maybe we can go diving together," Adrian suggested, before he truly thought about it. Adrian knew that was something that could never happen. The minute they went in the water, his tail would come back, and she would know. But he wished for it anyway.

"That actually sounds like fun." Isa grinned. "I'd love to."

Did I just ask her out on a date? Adrian realized that they were technically already on a date now, and the notion made him want to do backflips.

"Soon," he promised, though he wasn't sure how he'd be able to keep it. "I'll show you around some of my favorite diving sites."

Her eyes brightened. Her mood definitely seemed brighter from when he'd first seen her today.

They continued walking up the beach, and didn't stop until it ended at a rocky cove and they had to turn back. They talked, and talked, and each time the topic changed it seemed the two of them had more to say.

The day lengthened. Eventually, the sun started dipping lower and lower. Adrian didn't notice how late it was until he realized his shadow was lingering against the water. With it came a shocking pain he'd been ignoring, and a dryness in his throat that was practically unbearable. He'd been so wrapped up in their conversation he hadn't noticed the potion was wearing off. He'd have to go back into the ocean soon.

And leave Isa. The thought was terribly depressing.

"Shit. It's already getting late," Isa said. "I

hadn't realized. I really need to get home and finish my essay."

Adrian wilted, but he also knew it was time for him to go, too; his legs were getting really wobbly. He'd spent too long with Isa, though the day felt like it'd gone by in precious minutes. "I get it. We'll catch up later."

"Yeah, totally." Isa stopped and turned toward him. "Can I get your number? I'll give you a call."

"I, uh… I don't have a cell phone." He laughed nervously, and rubbed the back of his neck. "I'm not online, either."

"What kind of guy doesn't have a cell phone or social media?" She raised an eyebrow.

He laughed. "I'm not your average guy."

"Obviously." She looked him up and down, and Adrian felt himself growing hot all over. "Well… I guess I'll see you when I see you."

"It won't be long," he promised. "I'll be back to see you soon."

"How will you find me?"

"I'll know."

The red and orange of the sunset was mixing into the blonde of her hair, making her tan skin glow. She ran the tip of her tongue over her lips lightly, and it made Adrian hungry. Her eyes became hooded as he took a step closer, and their bodies were touching again.

"Isa…" he said, and he went to bend down. He lifted a hand to lay it upon the back of her hair.

Their noses were touching, and his lips were inches from hers...

Isa pulled away at the last moment. "I'm... I'm sorry," she finished lamely.

She wouldn't look at him, only down at the ground as she asked, "Do you need a ride?"

He shook his head. He was *so* disappointed. "No. I'll find my own way. Catch up with you later."

Isa nodded, then turned and ran up the beach like Adrian was chasing her. Adrian put his hands back in his pockets and shook his head.

"Water," he rasped. "I need to get back to the sea."

He couldn't transform here on this beach, not in front of all these people. But Adrian knew he had to get back to the ocean, and fast.

Adrian left that particular coastline and got back on the bus to be driven to his usual cove. When the bus pulled away from the ocean, Adrian clenched at his chest. The pain was so intense it felt like he was having a heart attack, and he struggled to breathe. His insides were shriveling up on themselves.

"Hey, buddy, you okay?" the driver asked as Adrian stumbled off the bus.

Adrian didn't answer. He proceeded downward, down the shoreline and to his cove. This time of day there was no one around, but Adrian worried it was too late. He could no longer breathe outside of water, and black dots coated his vision.

He picked up the pace. The water was directly

ahead, but that only made things worse, and he ended up gasping.

Adrian collapsed upon the line where the sea met the shore. His fingertips touched the ocean, and everything went dark.

ADRIAN CAME TO A FEW MOMENTS LATER. HE WAS suspended in the deep of the ocean, his tail was back, and Moona was looking closely at him in a way that signaled she was going to explode.

Everything *felt* fine now, but Adrian knew if Moona hadn't pulled him into the sea, it wouldn't have been. "Moona..."

Moona took a deep breath and belted out her rage. "How. Could. *You!?* You *know* better than to stay on land for that long, but you did it *anyway*! Then you left me to deal with questions from everyone on where you were! Do you realize how long it took for me to slip away, and how worried I was when I couldn't find you? I thought some human had broiled and fried you by now!"

"I'm sorry, Moona, okay? I couldn't help myself," he flung back at her. "I really don't need a guilt trip from you right now!"

"Don't give me an attitude. I saved your life," Moona snapped. "You would've suffocated onshore if I hadn't found you, and pulled you in!"

He knew she was right.

"Was it worth it, at least?" Moona snapped. "Did you find her?"

Adrian nodded. "I did, Moona. The mating bond snapped into place. She's mine, and I'm hers... at least, that's what the sea is telling me."

Moona relaxed. Her anger had changed to concern. "But... Adrian. She's a human, and you're a merman. How can you two be together?"

He shook his head. "I don't know. That's what I need to speak with my father about."

"*What!*" Moona's eyes popped out of her head. "You can't be seri- ous. Poseidon isn't going to allow this, Adrian. You know it."

"I have to try. The mating bond won't let me pick any other girl. It'll make me physically sick to be with anyone else. He won't have any choice but to accept it," Adrian insisted. "He's the god of the sea. My father must have *some* sort of magic that can fix this."

Moona fiddled anxiously with her fins. "He probably has something, but using it on you? I don't think he'll change you or her, even if you beg."

"I have to try." Adrian began swimming deter- minedly in the direction of Aquatica. "And who knows? Maybe he'll go for it."

Moona muttered something under her breath, but Adrian didn't hear her. As they swam back, Moona peppered him with pesky questions.

"What is it about her that you like so much? You barely know her," Moona said.

"I know, Moona." Adrian looked at her. "But I have this feeling in my gut about her that's so powerful. It goes beyond the mating bond. The way she rode that wave… you could tell she was fearless, that she was willing to live life on the edge. She wants a life of freedom, of adventure. And I want that too."

"You can't have that, Adrian. You're a prince. You have responsibilities," Moona said quietly.

Moona didn't understand. If she felt how he did, then she'd know.

Adrian couldn't help but feel nervous as he approached the palace's large silver doors, but the need to declare Isa his mate was stronger. He swam into the throne room, where a collection of merpeople gave him harsh glares. He wasn't very popular as the prince who'd abandoned his own party.

Poseidon was on the throne, but his mother was nowhere to be seen. Poseidon's rage grew as Adrian swam closer, but now wasn't the time for Adrian to lose his nerve.

"Father, before you say anything," Adrian said as the king opened his mouth, "Let it be known that I have officially found my mate."

Scattered claps were given throughout the court, although they were shocked and dispelled. Mermaids held their breath, waiting for Adrian's answer, and the court hung on every word.

The announcement that he'd found a mate was enough to dispel any irritation his father had stored for him. The grimace fell from the god's face, and he brightened immediately. "Well, that's wonderful news! No wonder you've been gone so long—you've been sneaking around with this mystery girl! Let's hear it! Who is she?" Poseidon pounded his trident against the floor.

"I'd prefer to speak with you alone, Father," Adrian said. "If that's all right."

Suspicion crossed the king's face. He supposed Adrian had chosen a commoner instead of someone from royal blood. The reality was much worse.

"Very well. Clear the room," Poseidon ordered, and merpeople reluctantly swam away. Mermaids cast glances over their shoulders, obviously hoping for good news for later.

"All right, son, don't hold your breath," Poseidon encouraged. "Give me the name of the lucky mermaid, and we'll get on with it."

Adrian took a deep breath. *Here it goes.* "Her name is Isa."

"Isa. Hm." Poseidon leaned back on his throne and stroked his beard. "I don't recall hearing that name before amongst our people."

"That's because she isn't a mermaid. She's a human."

Poseidon's casual demeanor vanished. His face darkened, and shadow grew around him as the water swelled and bowed. "What did you say?"

"You heard me." Adrian refused to be intimidated. "She's a human. And before you protest, yes, I've met her. I *know* her. She's the one."

Poseidon stared at his son for a moment or two,

like he was trying to comprehend what he was hearing. He didn't scream and rant as Adrian thought he would, and that scared him. Greatly.

"I knew I allowed this obsession with humans to go on for too long," Poseidon rampaged under his breath. "I figured it was a phase, a passing interest. I believed once you were older, you'd put these childish notions to rest."

"It's not a phase. I love her," Adrian rebutted.

"Love? What do you know of love, Adrian? How long have you known her, a few hours? Days, perhaps?" Poseidon challenged.

"You only knew Mother a single night before you declared her your queen," Adrian seethed.

"Your mother is one of us! This *human* girl is not!"

Poseidon had finally hit his limit. He lunged from the throne and stood before his son. "How did you meet her, by chance? She wasn't swimming in the middle of the ocean, no doubt."

"She was surfing. A wave knocked her over during a large storm— a storm you caused, may I add." Adrian's voice grew louder. "If I hadn't swam in and rescued her, she would've drowned!"

"You went to the surface? How *dare you* disobey my orders!" Poseidon seethed.

"Forgive me, Father, but I will be god of the sea someday. And I have to make my own decisions." Adrian fought back. He wouldn't allow his father to walk all over him, not when it came to Isa.

"Your decisions affect *our people*," Poseidon

raged. "You must think of more than just yourself! Every merperson depends on you to lead them, to make sacrifices for them!"

"She can become one of us. I know you have the power, Father. She can live among us in Aquatica, and—"

"Have you lost your mind?" Poseidon hissed. "Humans aren't to be trusted! If they knew of our existence, they would put us in labs! They would hunt us down to keep in zoos and aquariums. They would persecute us until none of us remained! Now you want to bring one of them down here?"

Poseidon's trident glowed. "No. I forbid it!"

"You cannot stop it. My heart has chosen her. The mating bond is already in place," Adrian said quickly.

"If she refuses your bond, the magic will force you to pick someone else," Poseidon argued. "That is what *must* happen. You shall choose another."

The thought of Isa turning him down gutted Adrian to the core. He knew it was a possibility. But he hadn't entertained the idea that she would say no to his hand, because it hurt too much. Her, a human, giving up everything she knew to live a life in the ocean with him? That was impossible.

But he refused to give up, even when logic pointed out the obvious.

"You don't understand. She's not like other humans. She cares about the sea, and what happens to it," Adrian argued. "She wants to help save it."

"One human is like the rest. They're all the

same." His father was taking back control. "I'll hear no more about it, Adrian."

"But—"

"No exceptions!" Poseidon's hand made a slashing motion through the air. "This cannot, and will not, happen! You will choose another for your bride, a *mermaid*, and put these childish fantasies aside! It's time you learned to act like a king instead of a boy!"

Adrian fell silent, and Poseidon turned his back on him. "Leave me. I'm ashamed to call you my son."

Adrian felt himself cringe. Fine. If his father wanted him to leave, he'd leave. He swam toward the great doors, but his mother was waiting outside of it. Ianthe stared at him, her face showing nothing.

"What about you?" Adrian asked harshly. "Am I a failure to you, too?"

Ianthe cupped the side of her son's face. "You must follow your heart, Adrian. To do anything else is to betray yourself."

Ianthe then swam away, toward Poseidon and his precious throne. His mother's words resonated deeply inside him, and Adrian made a decision.

When Adrian got back to his room he found it cleared of all human objects, even the gaming console he'd discovered a mere few days before. The space was practically empty. Moona was waiting for him, swimming in slow circles.

"I tried, Adrian," she said sadly. "But your

father ordered it all taken away. They wouldn't listen."

Adrian angrily punched the wall. He couldn't believe this was happening! It was more than unfair.

"What are you going to do, Adrian?" Moona asked him. She floated above him, looking down while Adrian pondered.

An idea came to him. It was a wicked idea—sinful. Wrong. He wasn't just betraying himself by thinking about it. He was betraying the entire kingdom.

But he was desperate. And desperation required the worst of actions.

"I'm going to see Stavros."

CHAPTER EIGHT

ISA

Isa couldn't believe she'd been such a coward.

She'd ran away from Adrian like a scared little girl, and she hated herself for it. He was going to kiss her, and she'd totally blown it. He probably thought she wasn't into him.

She'd hooked up with guys she'd known for a shorter time, but that hadn't been anything but messing around.

Adrian was different. She could tell he cared—feel it by looking into his eyes.

A morning class, a full day on the tour boat, and a half-shift at the aquarium should've meant she was too busy to think about Adrian, but that wasn't how it went. She found she was daydreaming most of the day about him... about his eyes, what color they were, and how his voice had sounded against the crash of the waves. Isa wanted to record it and replay the scenes over and over.

She'd probably seemed so pathetic to him. She told him she was busy because she didn't want to make it seem like she was desperate. But what Adrian didn't know was her schedule was so packed because she was desperately trying to fill the hole created by her father's absence.

She got a text from Harbor around nine. Brently Shores was throwing a beach party, a kegger to celebrate that his rowing team had made it to the semifinals.

Brently wasn't Isa's favorite person. He acted like he was a big deal, only talked about rowing, and had made it his personal mission in life to creep on her.

Ugh. Parties. They *so* weren't her thing. But she owed Harbor and Shelly for what she'd put them through the other night, so she said she'd go.

Isa slipped on a clean swimsuit with an orange cover-up, grabbed her flip flops, and headed out. She'd stay for an hour, have a few beers, and bug out.

She was tired. All she wanted to do was go to sleep and dream about Adrian.

She'd had the weirdest dream about him the night before. She dreamed they were swimming through the sea, and as she got closer, she saw he had a long tail... that there were fins on his arms, and gills in his neck. She'd dreamed that Adrian was a merman.

It was totally dumb. But the more Isa thought about it, the more she came back to what she'd seen on the boat— the green fin that had dipped underwater, and the face of the boy she thought had resembled Adrian's.

She pulled up to Brently's beach house and sighed. She was getting more delusional by the day. Hanging with Adrian made her realize how lonely she was. Maybe this party would be good for her.

The rap music was already blocking out the crash of the ocean, and a glow from a bonfire outside was illuminating the starry sky. There were so many people here, girls Isa hadn't seen since her high school graduation. There were more guys at the party than girls. They wore cut-off shirts with sandals and shorts, hats worn backwards and long hair wrapped into man buns. They crushed beer cans, made dirty jokes, and bragged loudly about how much they could lift.

Bros. *Double ugh.*

"Hey, baby. Glad you could make it!" one of them cried out as Isa passed them by. She cringed. She was on the way to find Harbor, but now she was forced to stop and turn around.

"What's up, Ken?" Isa forced a smile. "How've you been?"

"Not bad. Crossfit has been working out great. Want to touch?"

He flexed a muscle. Isa thought she might gag.

"No thanks. I'm actually seeing a guy," Isa blurted out, before she could stop herself.

"You're with someone?" Ken's eyes widened.

Isa had never dated anyone, more or less just

messed around. Ken was one of those guys she'd messed around with, and Isa wholly regretted it.

Ken wasn't a bad guy... but he wasn't good in bed, either, and his ability to hold a conversation was equal to his skills in biochemistry— non-existent.

"Yeah, I do. You don't know him. He's from out of town." She hadn't realized she'd thought of Adrian as her own. *Boyfriend* didn't seem like an accurate word. It was much more than that.

But that was crazy. She'd known him for so short a time.

"Hey, Isa." Luanne saddled up to Ken's side and put an arm around his waist. "Get any work done yet? You could use some Botox between your eyes. Wrinkles are starting to show, sweet thing."

Luanne was Ken's literal Barbie. Some girls were considered high maintenance, but Luanne was more expensive to keep than a pet leopard.

Isa had always thought Luanne looked fake. She always tried to make herself look like someone else instead of herself.

But if Isa was brutally honest, Luanne had spent all of high school trying to look like *her.* At one time, Isa had considered Luanne to be one of her best friends. She didn't know why now.

Isa was about to bite back that she was twenty and had no wrinkles, but she swallowed the come-back and said, "It's nice to see you, Luanne."

"You too, girl. You have a new man?" Luanne

smacked her gum. "Well, it's not like he'll last long. We all know how you go through guys."

Luanne threw her head back and laughed, and the crowd laughed with her.

Isa's cheeks burned. "I think it's different this time."

"Don't get your hopes up, sweetie. I'm looking forward to getting your sloppy seconds. You always nail the hottest guys." Luanne giggled, and Isa choked. The thought of her kissing Adrian made Isa want to reach out and strangle her, but she kept her composure.

"I'm gonna get a beer," Isa mumbled, and she turned back around, waiting to feel a knife in her back at any moment.

"She goes through men like money," she heard someone whisper.

"Daddy issues," the other person responded— like they knew.

There it was. Isa had to struggle to keep her fists at her sides as she headed up the steps. She had to find Harbor and Shelly.

Isa had drastically miscalculated. Being alone was less lonely than hanging around people you didn't like and had to be fake around. She'd been in college long enough she'd forgotten what wearing the mask was like, but her old high school friends were here, so she had to put it back on now.

Isa knew now. It was better to be alone and be yourself than to be surrounded by people who forced you to become a lie.

Inside, there were more people she knew from college than from high school, thank God. Harbor and Shelly were around the kitchen counter, taking Jell-O shots.

"Hey girl." Harbor was swaying. She was already drunk. She put an arm around Isa and bowed. "You're late."

Shelly hadn't started drinking. Already, as the mother of the group, she was taking care of Harbor.

"You okay? I know you didn't want to come," Shelly said in a low voice.

"It's fine," Isa said. "I wanted to see you guys, anyway."

"Shots, shots!" Harbor cried, shoving a few drinks toward Isa in a very pushy manner.

Isa had a few, but it didn't bother her. She had too high of a tolerance— lots of bingers in high school, times when she blacked out in order to forget who she was. She grabbed a beer, but merely sipped it… she was more hungry than thirsty.

For most of the night Isa followed Harbor and Shelly around. People were smoking and throwing up everywhere, and the house was a total mess. Isa didn't think Brently had cleaned up from the last party. There was beer pong, which Isa was a champ at, but she was uninterested. Isa really wanted to watch a movie or something… relax… but she knew people would that was lame, so she kept quiet.

She felt like she was too old for this. Like she'd outgrown all this, and the party was just a childish game people liked to play, to pretend like this was the best time of their lives.

This wasn't the best. The best was riding a killer wave, or feeling the sun on your face after a morning swim, or listening to a song you hadn't in a long time, or saving an animal at the aquarium her co-workers had insisted was a goner...

... And eating fresh crab on the beach with Adrian.

No. This party wasn't even close to that feeling. Isa closed her eyes and imagined it, tried to picture it in her head and pretended it was happening all over again.

She felt a thick arm squeeze her middle, and her entire body cringed. Her eyes snapped open to find Brently, King of Douches, with his arms wrapped around her.

"Haven't seen you around in a while, but I'd know that tight ass from anywhere," Brently slurred. "How you been, honey?"

Brently was the one guy in high school she'd never given a shot, and she didn't regret it one bit. But Brently was bitter he hadn't been given a ride. Even after all these years, he still wanted his turn.

He was the type of man who didn't understand no meant *no*. Which is why Isa made sure to never be alone around him.

Since she'd met Adrian, another guy brushing up against her seemed terribly wrong. This was downright unacceptable. Isa wrinkled her nose and said, "Haven't you heard, Brently? I'm dating someone."

She tried to bow out of his arms, but he held her tightly. Although they were in a room full of people, most of them were drunk, and the rest were Brently's friends. They'd let him get away with anything. With a terrifying start, she realized Harbor and Shelly had suddenly vanished.

"Who?" Brently demanded. "Who are you dating?"

"His name is Adrian. And if word gets out that you've got your arms around me—"

"Adrian? Never heard of him," Brently said dismissively. "You know they're going to elect me Coral King. We're gonna be perfect together."

If she heard about the Coral Queen contest one more time, she was going to scream. "I don't think so."

He bent down to spittle into her ear. "Come on, honey. You know you want me."

"You're gonna piss my boyfriend off. Leave me alone," she said, and she tried to shove him away.

Brently started dragging her toward his bedroom. "Come on, hon. Just one night. It's not gonna kill you. Everyone else has gotten a turn."

Aim for the groin. Isa brought up her knee to give him a kick, but before she could, she heard someone say in a dark, low tone, "Get off of her."

Brently let her go. Isa's eyes widened as she realized it was *Adrian.* He stood there, dripping wet from the sea, his clothes soaked and looking as though he'd swam across the ocean to get to her.

"Is this the asshole you were talking about earlier? I thought you just made him up," Brently said, jabbing an angry finger in Adrian's direction.

"Yes, actually." Isa crossed the room. She wrapped an arm around Adrian's waist and kissed his cheek. "He's my new man. So back off."

Adrian didn't have to say anything. His stare was enough to make Brently turn and walk away.

"Hey." Adrian turned and faced her, laying his hands on her hips. "Are you all right?"

"Yeah. Thanks for scaring off that creep." She breathed out a sigh, weaving a hand in her hair.

"You told him I was your boyfriend."

"I did." She felt herself blushing again. "Sorry about that."

He winked at her. "I don't mind."

People were staring at them. Adrian took her by the hand and said, "Let's leave."

They were stopped by Harbor and Shelly, who were lingering at the bottom of the stairs.

"Isa!" Harbor squealed. "Is this your new babe?"

Isa gave a weak smile. "Yep. Girls, meet Adrian."

"Adrian!" Shelly hiccuped. "Is this the guy you were talking about?"

"You've been talking about me?" Adrian asked. His grin only got bigger.

"Sure," Isa said, to answer both questions.

Harbor and Shelly gave each other eager looks, waggling their eyebrows.

The other girls were totally jealous. Adrian was definitely the most attractive man at this party, no questions asked, and once again, he was on Isa's arm. But this time, she was keeping him.

"Where do you want to go?" Isa asked as they passed the bonfire to leave the party.

Adrian opened his mouth to answer, but before he could, he was interrupted.

"She'll be gone in the morning, bud," a guy called out. "Never fall in love with a whore!"

Isa felt her insides seize. The voice had come from Hayden— a guy that had never gotten over when Isa had dumped him years ago.

She'd knew what people said behind her back. But no one had ever said it to her *face* before.

Adrian let go of her hand. He moved with such speed that his body became a blur. One moment he was next to Isa, the next, he wasn't.

People gasped when they saw Adrian with a hand on Hayden's throat, lifting him off the ground so that his feet were kicking. Adrian threw Hayden across the beach with such force that he crashed into the ocean a good twenty feet away.

People screamed. The crowd lunged back from Adrian as he turned around, faces marred with fear and panic. Isa's mouth dropped open.

Then... their faces cleared. The panic faded, their expressions going from scared to relaxed. The guests went back to the party as usual, laughing and chatting and enjoying themselves.

Hayden got out of the ocean, confused as to why he was wet. He stared at Adrian blankly, like he couldn't remember.

It was as if… as if nothing ever happened.

Isa was left speechless. That speed. The strength. It wasn't natural. No, more than that, it was less than unnatural… it wasn't even *human*.

Adrian was brooding when he returned to Isa's side. They got in her car. Isa didn't even care that he was wet and ruining her seat.

"Okay, what just happened back there?" Isa asked as she started up the car and began driving away.

"Nothing," Adrian said. "I took care of the problem."

"I was taking care of the problem! I was walking away," Isa said.

"No." His head snapped round to look at her. "People aren't allowed to disrespect you. I'm not going to stand for it."

Point taken, Isa thought, remembering how quickly Adrian had reacted. He nearly made it seem like it was a crime to insult her.

"How do you explain what happened? Everyone's going to remember you tossed Hayden like a football," Isa argued.

"They're all ridiculously drunk. They won't remember."

Adrian made excuses, and Isa knew they

wouldn't remember. She saw the look in their eyes. But it wasn't because they were too drunk. It was because Adrian had made them *forget.*

But how could she argue with him that he'd wiped the memories of everyone at the party? That was the kind of stuff that happened in lame television shows, not real life.

"Turn here," Adrian said, and Isa followed his instruction. "There's a dive I want to show you."

"How do you know more about Coral Bay than I do, and you're not even from here?" Isa asked.

Adrian gave a casual shrug. "What can I say? I get around."

Clearly. Isa hoped his *getting around* was more traveling and less physical.

Isa went through a drive-through, and Adrian told her to get grouper sandwiches. The smell alone was enough to make her stomach rumble.

They pulled off at the bay nearby and sat on the docks. Isa unwrapped her sandwich. It was a fried grouper on a warm roll, with mayonnaise, lettuce, and cheese.

She hadn't eaten anything all day. Isa bit into the sandwich, letting its salty flavor sting her mouth.

"Starving?" Adrian asked.

"I rarely eat," she said. "I'm too stressed."

"Well, that's going to change," Adrian said matter-of-factly as he shoved his second sandwich into his mouth.

They ate the grouper sandwiches on the bay while watching the ships come in. As they ate, Isa realized she really was oblivious to what happened in her little town. She and her friends always ate at the same restaurants, and visited the same places, over and over and over. They never tried anything new. Isa craved the unexpected, and rarely did she get it.

Adrian loved to explore. And that's what she liked about him.

"What's that?" Adrian asked, pointing to her ankle. Isa looked down. The dock light above them illuminated a tiny tattoo on her ankle, one of a mermaid with a purple tail and wavy blue hair.

"Oh, that? I got it on a dare," she said. "It was a long time ago."

"A mermaid?" He raised a brow playfully.

"I know it's kind of childish, but... I'm obsessed with mermaids." She shrugged. "I don't know. As a kid, I just thought they were cool."

"Well, mermaids are pretty badass."

She laughed. "Glad you think so."

"Who wouldn't?" Adrian spoke like everything she did was exceptional.

Not so much.

"More like... everyone." She sighed. "People think I'm a slut."

"Screw those people," Adrian growled. "Their opinions don't matter."

"It does, because they're right." She chewed the inside of her lip. "That's why you had to make

Brently let me go. He expects to get what everyone else has had."

"It doesn't matter if you've slept with the whole town. If you tell someone no, that's the bottom line," Adrian responded.

Isa pulled her knees to her chest. "I don't know. After my mom left, my dad stopped paying attention to me. He threw himself into work. I had to get the attention from *somewhere*, and guys were more than willing. I haven't slept with anyone in years, but people still remember everything I did in high school. This is my fault. I've made my own bed, and now I have to lie in it."

"It's never your fault if someone won't take no for an answer," he said quietly.

She leaned backward. "People don't think like that around here."

Adrian reached out his hand and placed it on top of hers. "Thanks for telling me the truth. And for what it's worth, I don't think it matters what happened in the past. Only what happens now."

"I'm tired of being a fake. I want to be honest," she replied. "I wasn't the nicest person in high school. I was kind of a mess. I want to change that and become someone better now. Turn over a new leaf."

"That's pretty honorable of you."

"I just want to do the right thing. I needed to start over." On instinct, she threaded her fingers through Adrian's.

He played with her fingers and asked, "So… boyfriend?"

She laughed lightly again. "I don't know. Maybe."

"Maybe?"

"Maybe." She caught him grinning at her, and she said, "Okay, yes. *Maybe* means you can be my boyfriend. Though it's all moving so fast."

"My mom says it's never too fast, once you meet the one."

That statement scared her, and Adrian seemed to know he'd gone too far. He let go of her hand and said, "You should probably get back home. I have to go."

"Where?" She stood up. "Why do you have to go, and so soon?"

"My dad's pretty pissed off at me. I snuck out. I'm not really supposed to be here," he explained. "If he finds out I'm not at home… well, he's gonna kill me."

She was disappointed, but she didn't want Adrian to get in trouble. "I get it. It's okay."

He walked her to her car. "Be safe out there, all right? Go straight home."

"You aren't my dad." She laughed. But it felt nice, someone caring about where she went.

"No, but you're my *girlfriend*, and I want you to be safe," Adrian said. It was so sweet she giggled again.

He put a hand on her arm and kissed her cheek. "Like I said, be safe. I'll see you soon. I promise."

Adrian made it sound like it was dire. But Isa knew he'd turn up again. Her cheek was warm when she got in the car, and she waved goodbye.

Isa started down the road, but before she got to the end of it, she turned around. She wanted to see Adrian one last time— give a better goodbye. She parked the car silently and got out, walking toward the docks.

Something inside told her to wait.

Adrian was at the end of the dock. He stared up at the moon, then down at the water. He pulled his shirt off with one fluid movement and tossed it aside.

He was going swimming. So what? Though she wished he'd invited her. There was no swimming allowed in the bay. That Adrian was a rule breaker was really attractive to her.

Then he started removing his pants.

Isa looked away— it wasn't right to stare at Adrian naked without his permission, even though he was acting *really weird*. Who knew she was dating a freak. It kind of turned her on.

A splash made her look up again. Adrian's clothes were left abandoned on the dock. She saw Adrian's upper half bobbing out of the water. Then he dived, and what Isa saw next caused her to fall backward in shock.

A green fishtail.

IT WAS ALMOST ONE IN THE MORNING WHEN ISA'S mind stopped whirling. She'd been lying in bed for hours, trying to deal with the undeniable truth. She'd found out everything she wanted to know, but she almost wished she hadn't. She could hardly believe it.

She wasn't sure why Adrian had pulled her out of the water that night, or how. She knew she didn't just wash up on the beach. With how big that wave was, she should've drowned.

It didn't make sense. How could Adrian be strong enough to swim through a storm like that and survive? No, not just survive... *save her life*, too?

He couldn't. Not unless he was born for it.

Isa knew there was something— or someone— lurking beneath the waves. It was then she was faced with a new reality.

Adrian was a merman. And there was a bond between them Isa couldn't explain— a bond she'd give her life for.

Isa made her mind up. She would confront Adrian about being a merman. Then she'd get some answers.

CHAPTER NINE

ADRIAN

Adrian swam toward Stavros' lair, more determined than he had ever been. The water was dark and murky that night, abandoned by an absent moon.

He'd had to see Isa one more time, just to be sure that this was the right thing to do. Seeing her at the party had only cemented it in his head this was the only option.

So she'd been with other guys. So what? It didn't bother Adrian. None of them mattered. She could've loved a hundred guys, but not one of them would ever compare to the love he had for her.

He'd wondered why she was so skinny. It bothered him that she wasn't eating. What she'd told him about her father… she was lonelier than he'd imagined. That kind of loneliness was painful for Adrian to fathom his mate going through. The sadness was so strong, he felt it from her, even at a distance.

Their bond was only growing stronger. Eventually, it would get to the point where Adrian would be forced to be with her... otherwise, he'd die just as quickly as if he was out of water.

Unless she refused him— which she wouldn't. The spell would hold. Adrian would change for her, become human, and she would accept him. This he forced himself to believe, because any other scenario was too painful to imagine.

Beside him, Moona swam, trying to talk him out of it.

"Adrian, this is crazy! Do you realize what he's going to do to you? Do you know what he's capable of?" Moona pleaded. True fear lurked in her eyes, and she reached out her fins to wrap them around Adrian's tail.

"Moona, let go. I've made my mind up." Adrian tried shaking her off, but Moona only held on tighter.

"I'm not going to let you do this. What he's going to ask for is a bargain you won't be able to keep." Moona closed her eyes and squeezed.

"Get off me." Adrian finally tore loose and increased his speed. "You heard what my father said. He won't help me. I have no choice. I *have* to do this."

"You can't change just for some... girl!" Moona burst. "Is it really worth giving up everything you've ever known, just to be with your mate?"

"This isn't only about Isa," Adrian demanded. "You don't get it. Even if Isa didn't exist, I *want* to live on land. I'm interested in humans, their technology, and how they live. Being in Aquatica is dreadfully boring. I want a new life."

"You say that now, but you're still so young. What happens if you get older, then regret the decisions you've made?" Moona argued.

"Maybe I could still go on living as a merman if my father agreed to let me go to the surface, without me having to sneak out." Adrian sighed. "But he's never going to understand. He *hates* that I'm interested in human life, and because he despises it so much, it makes me feel like he hates me, too. And this is a part of me — a big part — that I can't let go. I'm not going to sacrifice who I am to please my father. And if he can't accept me for me, I might as well not be in this family at all."

"But… if you become human, we might never see each other again," Moona said quietly.

"I know, Moona. And that's the worst part."

The closer they ventured to Stavros' lair, the less fish they saw. Eventually, the wide ocean became empty and changed color, from an opalescent blue into a murky green tinged with brown. Adrian held his breath as they swam through the water, and the cave of Stavros emerged.

It was a towering mount of dead coral that Stavros had elaborately fashioned into the shape of a castle, though no servants bustled around it. Stavros lived alone.

Adrian steeled himself for courage, but Moona whispered one last time, "Please, Adrian."

Adrian grabbed both sides of her face and looked her in the eye. "If there was another way, I would. But Moona... this is the only option I've got."

He kissed her forehead, then let her linger outside as he ventured into the cave. Moona peered around the edge and watched at a distance, her black eyes tinted with concern.

Adrian entered the cave. Inside, there were bottles of potions lining the walls, and jars filled with all sorts of disgusting ingredients... whale skin, fish eyes, bowels of sharks. Adrian gagged and tried not to look at them.

And bones. Bones of merfolk were littered throughout the cave floor, many of them still reaching for something Adrian couldn't see. Stavros had killed them while they were trying to fight back.

Adrian could see the glow of a cauldron at the end of the cave. Stavros was there, waving his hands over a green concoction that bubbled and brewed.

Stavros turned around, a wide smile on his face. "My boy." He spread his arms wide, like a loving uncle welcoming his estranged nephew home. "I knew you'd come by eventually."

Adrian swallowed. "You said I could come by at any time."

"And so you can." Stavros threw a living

octopus into the cauldron. "Though I'm not stupid enough to believe you're here to visit."

Adrian nodded. "There is something I want."

"And I suppose Daddy isn't strong enough to give it to you, so you came running to me." Stavros' smile only grew bigger.

"Can't. Won't. It doesn't make a difference," Adrian said. "Are you going to help me, or not?"

Stavros picked up his staff before settling on a chair made of bones, twirling his tentacles around his form. "That depends on what you ask for."

Adrian clenched his fists. This wouldn't be easy. He knew Stavros had the power to change him. He also knew that what he would ask for would be more than what Adrian could give. "I've found my mate. She's a human."

Stavros stared at him, before he began laughing. He wiped tears from his eyes and threw his head back.

"Oh, that's rich." Humor danced in his expression. "I suppose my dear brother wasn't too thrilled when he heard."

"No. He's demanding I pick someone else."

"But it's not that easy, is it?" Stavros asked. "A mating bond is powerful magic. Not easy to break, and devastating once it is."

"I don't plan on breaking it," Adrian said through clenched teeth. "I want you to turn me into a human."

Stavros' eyes instantly turned greedy.

"Hm." Stavros tapped his chin with one of his tentacles. "Interesting."

"What? Is it possible?" Adrian asked, growing impatient. "Do you not have the power?"

Adrian felt the water around him swell with heat as Stavros glared upon him, and he regretted saying anything.

"I have the power," Stavros said lowly. "There is more magic in me than what you could ever speculate in your wildest dreams."

"Great. Then let's get it over with. What do you want in exchange?" Adrian asked bluntly.

"I haven't asked for anything," Stavros said, feigning a shocked expression. "I would do *anything* to help my nephew."

Then, after a beat, he added, "In exchange for an alliance, of course."

"I won't make an alliance with you." Adrian had known Stavros would try to get him to turn against his father, but as angry as he was at Poseidon right now, he wouldn't betray his dad in that way.

Stavros sighed, and rolled his eyes. "You've always been so dramatic, Adrian. Fine. I'll make you a deal."

"Name your price." Adrian swam closer, so they were almost touching. "I'll pay it."

Stavros' grinned. He had Adrian right where he wanted him. "I'll turn you into a human for three days, and three nights. You have until then to convince your mate to fall in love with you... but you may not tell her that you love her, or say that you do if she asks. That's cheating. She must say that she loves *you* before the sun rises on the fourth day. Otherwise, you will turn back into a merman. Permanently. Never again will you be able to walk on land."

"*Never* again?" Adrian asked breathlessly.

"Never again." Stavros shook his head. "My magic will force you to remain a merman forever, no matter what spell you use or potion you take."

"What happens if she says that she loves me?" Adrian asked.

"You'll be a human permanently, and will be able to live the rest of your life happily-ever-after on land," Stavros said in a sickly voice— like the thought disgusted him.

Adrian paused. "But… if that happens, my father will be left without an heir. That means— the sea will pass to you."

"You are correct. If you are unable to assume the throne, on your father's passing, the sea will belong to me," Stavros said. "I will become the new Poseidon."

Adrian didn't like this. How could he turn his back on his people, even for his mate? If he agreed to these terms, he'd be betraying his father, and his kingdom. Everything he'd been raised to do would be for nothing.

But his father had turned his back on *him*. He had barely listened when Adrian had told him about Isa. Why should he care what happened to the kingdom?

"Okay. Let's just say, for argument's sake, she doesn't say she loves me. Then I'm stuck as a merman. What do *you* get out of it?" Adrian asked.

"Nothing." Stavros shrugged. "You will go on being your father's heir, and no doubt I'll be disappointed you didn't succeed. Though I can't say I won't revel in your failure."

Adrian didn't believe him. Stavros was hiding something. There was a secret in the magic.

Yet the offer was too good to pass up. He wasn't going to be a human any other way. "It's a deal." Adrian stuck out his hand.

Stavros couldn't contain his glee. He smiled so broadly Adrian was afraid he'd break his face. He clapped his hand into Adrian's and shook it roughly. "Yes! We've done it!"

The minute Adrian's hand connected with Stavros, he immediately felt sick. Stavros' black magic wrapped around his arm, squeezing his entire form. He let out an agonized sound as pain grew in his gut, spreading throughout his middle, his chest, his legs. The pain was so excruciating that Adrian couldn't move. He bent over and grimaced, shutting his eyes to the horrible sensations that were coursing throughout his body.

When he opened his eyes, Adrian looked down and realized he had two legs.

Adrian opened his mouth to let out a cry of joy, but the water that flowed inside his mouth choked him instead of revived him.

The water. His gills were gone. Adrian couldn't

breathe. He floundered for help and tried to swim, but he didn't know how to with legs. He'd never tried.

Stavros was laughing, and laughing. He didn't care Adrian was dying in front of him. He thought it was funny.

Hearing the commotion, Moona swam in. She knocked Stavros aside, and he stumbled into the wall. Moona pressed herself against Adrian, and he hung on for dear life as his friend pulled him along, hauling him to the surface.

Black spots dotted his vision. His lungs were screaming for air. Adrian felt like he was going to die… knew he was going to die. He clung tighter to Moona as the cave faded around him. The surface appeared so far above. They weren't going to make it.

But Moona wasn't going to let her best friend die, not on her watch, so she swam as fast as her flippers could carry her until she finally crashed against the line where the water met the sky. Adrian took a deep breath. He immediately started gagging, unsure of this strange new feeling that was coursing through him. Moona waited for him to catch his breath, supporting him with her weight.

When he was done gagging, his head lolled. Any moment, he was going to pass out.

Moona cried out something, but Adrian didn't hear her… *or couldn't understand her.*

His heart dropped. The change had taken place

so soon. He hadn't even been able to tell her goodbye.

Moona hauled Adrian across the ocean. It was a far swim from shore, but Moona paddled until her flippers were sore, slapping Adrian across the face with her tail to keep him awake.

Finally, the blessed line of the beach was in sight. Moona pushed Adrian toward it, going as close as she could without accidentally beaching herself.

Adrian pulled himself on shore, until he was out of the water completely. The earth rocked below him, and his head hit sand as he finally fainted.

CHAPTER TEN

ISA

Isa was walking on the beach that morning at sunrise, thinking about what she was going to say to Adrian the next time she saw him.

Those thoughts were completely erased from her mind when she realized Adrian was lying on the beach in front of her, passed out and completely naked.

Isa's first thought was how freaked out she was that Adrian didn't have any clothes on. She wondered if she should look away— if Adrian was going to sprout a fishtail right in front of her, or if she should turn and make a run for it. But on second glance… she really couldn't help it… Isa realized something was wrong.

He didn't look right. He looked — *dead*.

Isa immediately panicked. She rushed forward and fell to her knees at Adrian's side, trying not to scream.

Oh God. Oh God, oh God, he's dead. He's really dead.

Isa poked him, and his body shifted. A bout of hope rose in her chest as Adrian rolled over, opening his eyes and coughing.

"Adrian!" Isa said. She worried over him, not sure of what to do or how to help. "Are you all right? What happened?"

Countless scenarios swept through her head. This was insane.

"Clothes," he gasped, and he pointed at the cove in the distance. "There. Under — a rock."

Isa wasted no time. She ran to the cove and tiptoed around the sharp rocks that led inside the cave. Underneath a ledge were a pair of sandals, jeans, and a white tank top.

Isa ran back to the beach with the clothes in hand. She tripped twice on the way back to Adrian. He was on his hands and knees, trying to get up. Isa helped him. Adrian pulled his clothes on, though he needed Isa's arm to keep him steady.

She was worried about him. Yeah, she had to admit Adrian had a cute butt, among other things, but this was an *emergency here*.

"You need to go to the hospital," Isa said. This was a replay of what had happened to her, except now she was on the other side of it, and it was far worse.

"No," he gasped. "I'll be all right."

It was true. Adrian was recovering before her very eyes. She was about to ask Adrian why his clothes were so far away from him when she remembered that, as a merman, it would be obvious for him to hide clothes in a place nearby. It's not like he needed clothes in the ocean, right?

"What happened?" she repeated, feeling like a broken record.

"I went for a swim. Took in too much salt water," he rasped. "Good thing I washed up on shore."

Isa knew he was lying. But at the same time, she didn't want to question him when he looked like this.

"Are you sure you don't want to go to the hospital?" Isa repeated.

"I'm sure," Adrian insisted. He was able to stand on his own this time, without help. "Sorry you had to see me like this."

"I tried not to look at anything," Isa said, not wanting to make him feel uncomfortable.

"Doesn't bother me what you saw." Adrian smiled roguishly at her. "Thanks for helping me out."

"I couldn't just let you lie there," Isa said. "You had me super worried."

"I'm okay now." Adrian brushed his hair back. "What are you doing up so early? It's practically dawn."

"Couldn't sleep. I had a lot on my mind." She shrugged. "The beach helps me think."

"Me, too." Adrian stuck his hands in his pockets and looked out at the water. "Though not sleeping is a bad thing to do when you've probably got school and work to go to."

"I've got the next three days off, from work and school."

"Really? Why?"

"The Seaside Ball," she said glumly. "The whole town practically shuts down for it."

All her friends talked about was that stupid ball. It was in three days, and Isa had received an invitation. Not surprisingly, she'd been signed up for the Coral Queen vote. Isa didn't know the two other girls on the list, but she hoped whoever they were, one of them would get picked instead of her.

"Are you going?" Adrian asked. He raised an eyebrow.

Isa shook her head and looked down at the water. "I'm not sure. I'm *expected* to go. But I haven't really made up my mind."

There was an awkward silence, one Adrian broke out of necessity.

"I, uh… I need some more clothes," Adrian said. "I know it sounds weird, but I don't have any, besides these."

Yeah, because you wear scales most of the time instead of pants, Isa thought sourly, but she asked instead, "Where are your clothes?"

"It's a long story. But I don't have anything to wear and nowhere to sleep for the next few nights."

"You can stay with me," Isa blurted out. "I don't mind."

Adrian's eyes brightened. "Really? You sure that's okay?"

"Yeah," Isa said. "My dad won't notice you're there."

He really wouldn't. Having someone around besides Paola would be nice, for a change. Adrian would be a blast to hang out with.

"We can go to the mall," Isa suggested. "I have cash."

"I'm not going to make you pay," Adrian said, as if it offended him. "Wait here."

Adrian went back to the same cove Isa had gotten his clothes from. He came back with a wallet that was stuffed full of bills.

"I have a ton of money," Adrian said when he caught her looking. "I just never use it."

Hm. A ton of *human* money. He had resources, despite being a merman. His dad must be very important. Which reminded her...

"What does your dad do again?" Isa prodded as they walked back to her car. "I don't remember."

"I didn't really tell you." Adrian had gone quiet. "It's a family business, like I said."

"Oh, really?" Isa left the question open-ended, so he was forced to answer.

"He's... a boss. He tells people what to do all day. It's really not my thing," Adrian mumbled.

So his dad was some sort of ruler of mermaids. Which had to make Adrian a prince. Isa's dreams were practically coming true.

Hold on, Isa. Princes don't just wash up naked and

perfect on the beach for girls to find. There has to be a catch. Isa decided that by the end of their extended weekend, she'd find out exactly what was the downside to Mr. Wonderful himself.

When they got to the mall, Isa figured Adrian would want to go to all the high-end stores, but Adrian was stuck to tank tops in different colors, shorts and jeans, and ignored accessories entirely. He thought hats were dumb, though Isa insisted he'd want one to keep his head out of the sun.

"You know, most dudes I know wear expensive clothes to show off," Isa said as Adrian grabbed another plain tee. "You know. Logos. Name brands."

"I'm not a flashy kind of guy. Who do I need to show off for?" he asked.

"Girls," Isa said instantly. "All the guys I know are obsessed with impressing girls."

"There's only one girl I want to impress, and she doesn't care about clothes," Adrian told her. He tweaked her nose, and Isa smiled.

They had their first official argument as boyfriend and girlfriend when it came to pick out swimwear.

"I don't like wearing swim trunks." His nose wrinkled as Isa held up a pair of trunks, decorated with black palm trees against an orange sunset.

"Clearly not, as you were tanning on the beach buck-ass nude this morning. And it's Florida. You need a swimsuit. You *want* to show everyone the boys?" Isa asked as she shoved the suit in his face. "Because *I* don't want anyone to see them."

Anyone but me, that is. He's mine.

Isa wasn't sure where this sudden emotion had come from. She hadn't been the jealous type before, but it was a whole new story with Adrian.

Adrian snatched the suit from her. "Fine. If you insist."

He definitely wasn't bashful, but that didn't mean Isa was slipping out of her bikini for him anytime soon.

They stopped to eat at a food court when lunch rolled around. She shared an order of orange chicken with him they got from the Chinese takeout place.

Isa rifled through a celebrity magazine someone had left behind while they ate. She stopped when she came upon a picture of a woman with long hair the color of a sapphire. It was a scandal she'd changed her hair in Hollywood to such an outrageous color.

If a celebrity couldn't get away with it, Isa knew she couldn't, either.

"There a secret message on that page or something?" Adrian teased.

She looked up. "It's kind of a secret. Don't tell anyone, but I've always wished I had blue hair."

"Really?" Adrian seemed surprised.

"Yes. Like the ocean. I've always wanted to dye it, ever since I was fourteen."

"Why haven't you?"

"My friends thought it was dumb. They said they'd laugh at me." Isa blew a strand of blonde hair out of her eyes. "Plus, my dad would kill me. Fun isn't allowed."

"I think you would look beautiful with blue hair. Where I come from, girls have hair of all colors," Adrian said.

Yeah, underwater, not on land. Yet Isa still stared at the photo wistfully. She wanted and wanted.

Adrian grabbed her wrist. "Come with me."

Somehow, she ended up in a salon chair in the nicest dye bar in the mall. Isa tried to explain to the excited stylist that no, she wasn't going to dye her hair blue, no matter what her overbearing, rich and enthusiastic boyfriend said, but the more Isa tried to refuse and the more color samples the stylist showed her, the more Isa felt her reserve weakening.

This was something she'd wanted to do since she was a teenager, and she'd never allowed herself to do this one small thing, just for her. What would be the big deal if she *did* change her hair color? Why did it matter, and why did everyone care so much?

More than that... why did their opinions matter?

Isa had the thought that nobody would elect a girl to Coral Queen who had blue hair. That's when she finally said yes.

Two hours later, Isa emerged from the salon feeling like she could conquer the world. Her blonde hair had officially been changed to a vibrant and eye-catching blue. It had an ombre effect, and started as a light sky-blue at the top before fading to turquoise, then a rich sapphire at her ends. When she moved it back and forth, her rippling locks looked like a wave and shone against the light. Isa had never felt more confident in her entire life.

Adrian was outside a gaming store, looking at an Atari that was on display. When he turned around and saw Isa, he had the biggest smile on his face.

"You. Look. Amazing." Adrian put the shopping bags down and picked her up, spinning her around. "I'm so glad I talked you into this."

"I'm glad you did, too."

Isa ran a hand through her hair again. She couldn't stop touching it. "It's like... I feel like *me* for the first time ever."

"I'm glad to hear that." Adrian took her hand, and they walked through the mall together.

Adrian caught her looking at girls coming out of a prom dress shop across the aisle way. "You want to go in?"

"What? Me. No. Prom's long over for me." She laughed.

But before she'd even finished her sentence, and in a dressing room. Isa had grabbed the first dress she saw as a whim, just to try on for fun, but the moment she slipped it over her body, Isa had a feeling that she'd just put on the dress of her dreams.

The dress was a color that matched her hair, and was covered in sequins that looked like scales. It was a mermaid fit, and clung to the top and middle of her body before fanning out around her feet in a mess of tulle and sequins.

She felt like she was covered in blue diamonds. She looked like some sort of mermaid princess. Isa had fallen in love with it. She exited the dressing room to show Adrian. His face lit up the moment he saw her.

"It would be worth it to go to the ball if I was wearing a dress like this," Isa said, spinning around.

"Why don't you?" Adrian got up and took both her hands in his. "If you want, I'll go with you."

"Is that your way of asking me to the dance?" She put a hand on her hip. "No soliloquy, no song or flash mob? Chivalry is dead."

Adrian laughed, got down on one knee, and asked, "Isa, will you be my date to the Seaside Ball?"

"Okay, yes, yes, shh," she told him, giggling as she yanked him up. "You're making a scene."

And he was. People were looking at them, but she didn't care. Going to the ball wouldn't be so bad if Adrian was her date.

Besides, she couldn't wait to see everyone's expressions once they saw she had blue hair. They'd totally freak out.

Isa decided the Seaside Ball would be her new beginning. She'd finally come out as herself, and show the world who she really was. She'd rub it in everyone's preppy faces that she was never the girl they thought she was, but someone *more.*

When they left the mall and got back into her car, Isa pulled something out of the shopping bags — something she'd bought in secret.

"This is for you, Adrian," she said, and she unwrapped the Atari. "I got it behind your back when you weren't looking. It's my way of repaying you, for my hair and the dress."

"You didn't have to repay me," Adrian said, though he was clearly in awe. He was geeking out over the old system.

"No, seriously." She pressed the console into his hands. "I saw you obsessing over it earlier. This is a thank you, for everything you've done for me."

Adrian grinned. "You don't know how much this means, Isa. I literally just lost one of these."

"Well, now you have it back." She smiled at him and started the car. "Come on. Let's go home and play it."

CHAPTER ELEVEN

ADRIAN

Isa's house was really big. Way bigger than Adrian expected.

He wondered how she was able to stand it, being so alone so often in such a big place. The palace was larger, but there were always hundreds of merpeople swimming about it to keep him company.

Here, it looked like the only person who lived here was Isa.

Isa had walked all around the huge complex, calling for her father. No one answered.

"Hm," she said when she returned to Adrian, who was leaning against a counter in the kitchen. "That's strange. He should be home by now."

"Your father is gone for the weekend, *chica*," someone called. A small woman walked into the room. She screeched when she saw Isa's locks "Isa, what did you do to your hair?"

"I dyed it. Do you like it?" Isa asked hesitantly.

"I *love it*!" The woman hugged Isa tightly, and Isa beamed. "It suits you perfectly."

The woman's smile brightened once again when she saw Adrian. "Oh? And who is this?"

"Paola, this is Adrian, my boyfriend." Isa took Paola by the shoulders. "Adrian, this is Paola. She... well, she helps me a lot."

Adrian wasn't sure what that meant, but he didn't have time to reason, because Paola was already throwing her arms around him and kissing him on the cheek. "How lovely! Isa hasn't had a boyfriend in so long! And so handsome, too!"

"Where is my dad, Paola?" Isa asked with a laugh, breaking them up. She practically had to pry Paola off of him.

"Oh, he was called away for the weekend. Something about work," Paola told her, and she frowned. "He'll miss the Seaside Ball. I'm sorry."

Isa's face remained passive. "It's fine, Paola. Thanks for telling me."

"Do you want me to stay and cook you something? Dinnertime willbe in an hour," Paola said with a glance at the clock.

"No, it's fine. We were just going to order pizza, anyway. Go home and relax."

Isa shooed Paola away and closed the door behind her.

Isa looked so small up against the doorway. She was waiting any moment for Adrian to pounce on her like a tiger, expecting him to start groping her now that they were alone in her house.

That wasn't his style.

He raised the Atari. "You promised me we would try this."

Isa relaxed. "Yep. Come on, living room's this way."

The TV in the living room was bigger than Adrian had seen in some movie theaters. He'd always loved televisions, but he never got to do anything as fun as play an entire video game, or have a movie marathon. Electronics didn't work underwater, and he'd always been cursed to only a few hours at a time on land.

Now that time was unlimited, and the prospect of that amazed him.

Isa set up the Atari, and they started to play. Immediately, she noticed how incredibly bad he was at gaming.

"I thought you were like some video game freak, the way you geeked out over that Atari," Isa told him suspiciously.

He shrugged, but the smile was broad on his face. "You can like something without being good at it."

Truth was, he was still learning the buttons.

When the pizza showed up Adrian was thrilled to see that she'd ordered anchovies and crab as toppings instead of pepperoni. Meat from land animals never went well on his stomach.

"Sorry it's gross, I didn't think—" she started,

then went quiet as she watched Adrian shove a whole piece into his mouth.

"Say no more." He grabbed another piece. Isa laughed and didn't ask any questions.

They played the Atari until it was almost dark, then Isa turned on cable. "My favorite show is on," she told him. "I never miss it. I hope you don't mind."

"I don't care. Watch what you want." He shrugged.

"That's such a guy response." She went into the kitchen to make popcorn, and Adrian watched the previews for the show as the last program finished up. Isa's favorite sitcom was some sort of fantasy soap opera about mermaids. How did he guess?

Isa plopped onto the couch with a full bowl of popcorn and sat it between them. She leaned against him as they ate. Adrian noticed that she'd changed her shirt to a low-cut top, and was leaning further forward than she had to.

She was testing him... seeing how far he'd go. Adrian wasn't about to be tempted. Everything rode on this going well, and he wasn't messing it up.

Isa got the hint that nothing was going to happen halfway through the show, and moved to the other side of the couch. She splayed her legs out like she didn't care about looking feminine or attractive, which made Adrian feel much better.

"This is really nice," she said. "I haven't had a day to just chill in a while."

"Don't you do this with your friends?" Adrian asked.

"My friends would think this is boring. They just want to party all the time. They expect me to be something I'm not." She played with a popcorn kernel.

Adrian couldn't imagine anything being boring, so long as Isa was around. "People put expectations on me, too," he said. "I'm not who everyone wants me to be, either. Where I'm from, people consider me... weird. I'm not like everyone else."

Isa tossed a piece of popcorn at him, and he jumped up off the couch to catch it in his mouth. She giggled. "Well, maybe we can be weird together."

"I would like that." Adrian grabbed a piece of popcorn and tossed it. "Catch!"

Isa tried to nab it with her mouth, but she fell over the side of the couch instead. She laughed when she hit the floor, and said, "Try me again!"

They spent the rest of the night tossing popcorn back and forth, seeing how difficult they could make it to catch. That led to a strange game of *Jaws*, where Adrian was the shark and Isa the dying swimmer, which *then* led to making a fort out of pillows, couch cushions, and blankets.

"I haven't done this since I was a kid," Isa said when she finally put the last blanket in place. She crawled underneath the fort, to where Adrian was waiting. They lied next to each other side by side on their stomachs. "But don't you think we're a little old for this? It's childish."

"Do you care what people think about you? About us?" he questioned.

He knew he didn't give a shit. Screw the world. The only thing that mattered anymore was he and Isa.

"I... I think I have, for a long time," she said slowly. "But I'm kind of tired of it. And I don't think I want to care anymore."

Her face was very close to his. Adrian leaned in so they were closer, and at this point, he couldn't stand it any longer. The TV was still playing in the background, and the light reflected waves off her blue hair. He pressed his lips to hers softly, and kissed her like he imagined the ocean kissed the sand, or like the sunset did the sky as it went over the horizon.

Isa seemed surprised, before she dove into his kiss and gently returned it back, closing her eyes and allowing herself to float easily upon the surface before swimming within its depths.

When Adrian pulled back, things seemed tense between them. Isa went to move away, and he didn't like it.

"You can sleep in my bed with me, you know," Isa offered. "My dad's not coming home. We aren't going to get caught."

That's what she was worried about? Adrian had other things on his mind. "I don't want to make you feel uncomfortable."

"We're boyfriend and girlfriend, aren't we? That's what couples do."

Isa tried to crawl out of the fort, but Adrian snagged her wrist before she could get away.

"I don't want to be *that* kind of boyfriend," he told her. "I want to know the real you. And I want to make this last a long time."

The expression on her face was hard to read, but even so, Adrian could. She wasn't used to commitment. Actually… it seemed like Isa wasn't used to anything more than a quick one-and-done.

He was going to change all that.

Isa leaned against his shoulder as the show continued to play. Adrian didn't know how late it was. They'd been playing around for hours. The kiss had made time come crashing back into reality.

A short time later, he heard snoring. Isa had fallen asleep in the fort. He didn't want to wake her.

Adrian turned on his back, laid his head on a pillow underneath him, and looked up at the blanket ceiling. His legs were tingling, and he felt odd. It was weird to him, not having a tail. Already, he longed for the ocean. He wanted to feel his fins, not his feet.

He didn't expect to miss being a merman. He thought he'd left all that behind him.

But it was too late to back out now, and Adrian didn't regret his decision.

Three days was a ridiculously short time to humans. Adrian hadn't considered that. There were humans who had been together three years who still hadn't told one another they loved each other. How could he expect Isa to say that she loved him in such a small period of time?

The first day was almost over, and Adrian felt that Isa was no closer to saying she loved him than the day before.

Already, he had so little time.

CHAPTER TWELVE

ISA

When Isa woke up the next morning curled up against Adrian's side in their little fort, she realized how happy she was.

But this whole thing with Adrian was a little *too* perfect, and it bothered her. He was a gorgeous guy, and despite everything she'd tried last night he hadn't made a move, not even after they'd kissed. He even refused to sleep in her bed.

They acted like little kids together, and she loved it. It was fun. There was no pressure and no need to feel grown up. Being with him was so easy.

He had to be a serial killer or something, because this was too good to be true. Were mermen serial killers? There had to be at least one.

Isa thought about confronting Adrian about being a merman. But she didn't want to ruin the fairy tale, not yet, because if Adrian was hiding something, bringing it up might make him go away. So she ignored the thought and went on with her day.

Isa got made breakfast, bacon and eggs with pancakes. At the smell of food, Adrian came into the kitchen. He seemed as happy as she was. They didn't talk, but while they were eating, Isa noticed Adrian only touched the pancakes and avoided the bacon and eggs.

"So what are we doing today?" Adrian asked as he finished up.

"I got a new board," Isa said. "I was hoping to try it out."

"I've never been surfing," Adrian said. "It'd be cool to learn."

"I think I have an old board around here you can use." Isa ruffled through the mall bags from yesterday and tossed him his swimsuit. "Get dressed, and let's go."

Isa said screw the shower and threw on her bikini. She met Adrian by her car, and they headed down to the beach.

Isa half-expected Adrian to grow a tail the minute they were waist- deep in water, but she looked down, and saw he still had legs. Could he control what he looked like? Adrian hung onto the board warily, looking a bit confused.

"What do I do?" he asked.

"Watch this." Isa waded into the water, where a small wave was growing. She hopped up on her board and crouched, then rose to her feet slowly as the wave grew stronger. She easily rode it in a casual, careless way. She could feel Adrian's eyes on her as she floated back to where he was.

"You're a natural out there," he told her. "It's like you were born to surf."

"The sea is where I belong," she told him. "I've known that since I was a little girl."

She was glad the sea was calm today, because Adrian had no balance. If he could barely stand upright on land, there was no way he could handle being on a board in the ocean. Each fall was more floundering and spectacular than the last.

Isa was happy Adrian was here with her. If he wasn't, she probably would've spent the three-day weekend alone. She was used to being alone, and didn't mind it, but it got boring after a while.

"I really suck at surfing," Adrian said after he'd taken his twentieth fall, one where he'd knocked the corner of his board. "I should be banned from it permanently."

"You're not that bad. Everyone's terrible their first time," Isa said, though she wasn't being honest. Adrian really was awful.

"We should do something I'm good at," he said. "Also, something that involves being out of the sun, because personally, I'm boiling out here."

"What did you have in mind?" Isa asked curiously.

Adrian tilted his head. "Do you have snorkeling gear?"

"Is your uncle going to kill you for this?" Adrian

yelled over the roar of the engine.

Isa grinned. "I've been a good girl lately. I think he worries I'm behaving a little too well."

Adrian laughed. Isa steered the boat, but Adrian came up behind her and put his arms around her, wrapping them tightly against her form as she held the wheel.

"It's this way," Adrian said. "No one but me knows where it is."

Isa grew warm inside at Adrian's comforting form around her. He steered the boat with her until land disappeared, and he told her to drop anchor.

"It's here," he said, and he handed her goggles and a snorkel. "I come out here all the time. It's beautiful. The best part is I don't think anyone has found it yet."

Adrian dove in. Isa fitted the goggles to her face and followed him, leaving the snorkel in her hand for now.

What Isa saw beneath the surface took her breath away. A coral reef stretched on for miles below, a dazzling display of rocks and sea plants that were green, blue, pink, purple, and an assortment of other colors. The reef touched the ocean floor hundreds of feet below the surface and went on for as far as she could see. Adrian gestured for her to follow, and she did eagerly.

All kinds of fish swam in the reef. King mackerel swam next to red snapper, and there were swordfish that were as big as she was. Crabs scuttled along the coral next to tuna, catfish, grouper, and even blowfish. Isa counted a few stingrays swimming majestically up and around the towers of coral. She even saw dolphins swimming in the distance.

It was an entire world of its own, and nobody on earth even knew it was here. Nobody, except for her and Adrian.

Adrian and Isa swam to the surface. When their heads broke the water, Isa had to gasp for breath.

"Aren't you worried about sharks?" Isa asked. She knew there had to be tons swimming about, this far in the ocean and with so many fish around.

"Sharks won't bother us. Trust me," Adrian told her.

Why, because you're some king of the sea? Isa decided to trust him. If he and his merman powers were enough to keep sharks at bay, it was good enough for her.

Isa noticed that Adrian had trouble swimming in the water… like he didn't know how to use his feet. His spine slithered up and down in a wave-like motion instead of staying still, and his legs and arms flapped in the water. He was barely keeping himself afloat.

He obviously doesn't know how to swim without a tail, Isa thought. She kept a close eye on Adrian, to rescue him just in case he went under. After all, she wasn't sure if the poor guy still had gills.

Adrian and Isa snorkeled along the surface to look down at the reef, occasionally diving to get a closer look. Once Adrian grabbed her hand and took her under, close to a school of fish. He kissed her underwater as the fish swam around them. Isa quickly had to swim to the surface, to recover her breath from such a beautiful moment.

As the day grew late, Isa noticed a gray shape bobbing along the surface of the water.

"Hey." She nudged Adrian. "What's that?"

Adrian peered over her. "That's Moona," Adrian said. "She's my friend."

Cautiously, Adrian approached the figure. Isa dipped underwater for a second to see that the creature was a manatee.

What was a manatee doing this far out? They liked the warm water near the shores. The manatee swam closer until it was between them. Her big black eyes were lovely. She seemed gentle, but curled around Adrian in a way that made Isa think she was jealous.

"You can pet her," Adrian said. "She won't mind."

Moona's tail rose out of the water to slap down, and the splash hit Adrian in the face.

Isa reached out to touch Moona, before she pulled her hand back at the last second. Manatees were endangered creatures, and shouldn't be messed with.

But then Moona did something unexpected. She floated forward and wrapped her fins around one of Isa's legs, giving it a light hug.

"Look!" Isa cried in excitement. "I think she likes me!"

If Adrian could do backflips in the water, he probably would've. "That's a relief. Moona's not very nice to people she doesn't like."

Isa noticed the thick white scars lacing across her back. "Boats," Adrian said when he caught Isa looking. "She's been hit by them a few times."

"You poor thing. I'm sorry." Isa held out her palm, and Moona brushed her whiskery lips across Isa's fingers before she turned and floated away. The manatee gave Adrian a peculiar look as she went, though Isa thought she was imagining things.

The sun was growing lower in the sky. Isa was tired from being in the water all day; and she was certain that Adrian felt worse due to all his poor swimming. Adrian said, "It's getting late. Let's go back."

"I don't want to," Isa said. "It's so incredible out here. I want to stay forever."

"Maybe one day, we'll never leave." Adrian guided Isa back to the boat. He helped her on once he'd climbed aboard, and Isa drove the boat back to land.

She caught Adrian staring at the expanse of water behind them. "You miss it, don't you?" she asked. "The openness of the sea."

Adrian held on for a moment, before he sighed. "I didn't think I would. But I actually do."

Neither of them had discussed what he was. Before this moment, Isa was certain Adrian had no idea she knew the truth.

Now, she wasn't so sure. Every minute, every

second they spent together was bringing them closer. And it hurt Isa that he kept hiding secrets from her, though she was certain now Adrian had to suspect she realized the truth.

As they rolled at a lazy pace back to shore, Isa felt a rough bump, one that shook the boat. She brought it to a screeching halt and looked down, trying to see what she'd hit and hoping it wasn't poor Moona.

She only witnessed it for a second. He was there, and then, he was gone. It was a man... a thin-faced one with a goatee. There was a flash of tentacles... then nothing.

"Adrian, I think there's a person down there," she told him.

He was already at her side and looking very pale.

"I think we should go down and investigate," Isa insisted.

"No," he said immediately. "It was probably just a reef you hit."

"I saw a man's face, and tentacles," she said. "I'm pretty sure it wasn't a squid. We should put on our snorkeling gear and take a look."

"It was *nothing*, Isa," he snapped. "You're seeing things. Let's go back."

Adrian's reaction had only confirmed whatever she'd seen hadn't been a squid at all. Someone in the ocean was watching them.

Isa decided it was time. Tonight, she'd confront

Adrian about being a merman. From there, she'd see where they stood.

CHAPTER THIRTEEN

ADRIAN

Stavros was watching them. That Adrian was certain of.

Adrian wasn't worried about Poseidon looking for him, because it wasn't unusual for him to slip off for days at a time. They'd gotten in a fight, so his dad probably assumed Adrian was mad and off hiding somewhere. He wouldn't know his son had left Aquatica for good until it was too late.

But Stavros was a different story... he had a seahorse in this race. He couldn't keep track of them on land, but once they were in the ocean, his uncle's eyes were on him. That meant he would have to keep Isa out of the water as much as possible for the rest of the time he had with her.

A nearly impossible task, seeing how much she loved the sea.

He knew taking her out to the reef would be a risk. But he'd wanted to share his favorite place with her so badly. He hoped they wouldn't be there that long, but they'd been out in the water for hours. Stavros had probably been lurking around for some time, seeing how close Adrian was to achieving his goal.

But Adrian didn't know if he was. They'd kissed a few times, and she'd been impressed by the reef, but the L-word hadn't been mentioned. Adrian didn't even know if it was on the table.

He loved Isa. But did she feel the same?

Her uncle wasn't too happy when they returned with the boat, but he didn't yell at her. It seemed Isa had a way of charming everyone she met. She treated that gift like a curse instead of a blessing.

"Hey, Adrian," she asked when they hiked back to her car. "I have a request."

"Name it,' Adrian said. He'd do anything to win her over.

"I want to sleep on the beach tonight," she said. "Have a bonfire, maybe grill some stuff. The sound of the waves helps me think, and sleeping under the stars just sounds... romantic."

It did, kind of, but Adrian wanted to know what she was getting at. "There's a spot I know where we won't be bothered."

Gathering supplies took longer than either one of them thought it would, because when they got back, Adrian wanted to play his Atari, and while grocery shopping, they couldn't agree on what to grill. Isa wanted hamburgers and Adrian, of course, insisted on fish, so they agreed to disagree and got different things.

It was past eight and the summer sun was setting when they finally made it back to the beach. Adrian took Isa to his secluded spot by his cove and started a fire, while Isa laid a collection of pillows and blankets on the sand. She burned charcoal on the portable grill they'd brought, and when the grill was finally hot enough, Adrian tried to show off and told her he'd do the cooking.

It was a disastrous idea. The food was blacker than the charcoal when Adrian got through with them. Isa laughed and took over, making dinner herself. By the time they finally ate, the moon was rising and stars had already dotted the expansive navy sky.

"It's so peaceful out here," Isa said, sighing with contentment. She lied back against the blanket, and said, "There's nothing I love more than the smell of the sea. It's like you can almost taste the salt water."

"Nothing?" Adrian smiled.

"Maybe the feel of a board, and riding a wave." She tossed her hair over her shoulder. "I don't need much. Despite what everyone says about me being high maintenance."

"What do you want out of life, Isa?" he asked curiously

"A shack on an island. One where I'm preferably left alone," she said under her breath.

She'd said something similar before. Adrian moved closer to her. "I don't think you mean that."

She put her head against his shoulder. "Don't take it that way. You're not like anyone I've ever known."

"Isn't that a good thing?"

"It's a hell of a good thing. I'm happier for it." The fire crackled, and she said, "But, Adrian... I think I need to ask you something."

Was this it? He hoped she didn't ask if he loved her. He couldn't tell her that, or the spell would break. "What is it?" he asked, heart pounding.

Isa swallowed. "I know what you are. And I don't think it's fair for you to hide it from me anymore."

Adrian went into full-on panic mode. "What do you mean?"

"Don't play dumb. I saw you change the day at the docks. You're a merman."

Adrian's innards bottomed out. "I'm..."

"Please don't lie." Isa turned to face him. "I get why you wouldn't tell me. I mean, it's kind of crazy, isn't it? But I want to know more about you. I know I saw you in the water on my uncle's tour boat, and I've figured out the only way you could've saved me after I nearly drowned that day was if you could swim better than a human could. But we've been in the water all day, and I haven't seen you change once. What's going on?"

Adrian swallowed. "Okay. You figured it out... I'm a merman."

Isa's face went from certain to unsure. Disbelief crossed her eyes, like she couldn't believe her crazy theories were actually true. She pointed at the water. "Show me," she said. "Show me your tail."

"I can't," he said. "It won't work."

"Are you playing a prank on me?" Isa's face grew slightly pink. "Because if you are, it's really messed up."

"No." He grabbed her hands. "I swear on my life, I'm telling the truth. But I can't change right now, because I made a deal with a sea warlock to become human."

"Why would you do that?" she whispered. "You had everything. You were mythical. You could live in the sea forever. Why would you want to come on shore and be with humans?"

"Because, after I saved you, I really wanted to spend more time with you. And the only way I could do that is if I had legs, not fins. In my merman form, I can change into a human for a short time, but it wasn't enough. A few hours goes by like seconds when I'm with you. I needed more time."

"When I found you on the beach... did you make the deal then?" Isa wondered.

Adrian nodded. "Yes. Moona brought me to shore. She saved my life."

Isa hesitated. "Who did you make a deal with? Was it the person I saw in the water today?"

"Never mind," Adrian said. "They're far away from us now."

"Adrian... what did you have to give up to be with me?"

"It's not important," he said quietly. "I couldn't tell you even if I wanted to. You know the stories of Poseidon, the god of the sea?"

"I'm not familiar with much Greek mythology," she said. "But, yeah."

"I'm his son."

Her mouth dropped open. "No way."

"I *swear* that it's true. And I know this sounds insane, but you have to believe me."

Isa stared at him with big, green eyes. Adrian was certain she was about to call him a liar and leave him stranded on the beach, but all she said was, "Okay. I believe you."

"Thank you." The words came out in a whoosh of breath.

Isa stared at him. "Did you really want to be on land that badly?"

"I wanted to be with you more than anything," Adrian confessed. "I couldn't do that without making a sacrifice."

"I'm sorry you miss the ocean. Is it permanent?"

"I don't know." Adrian hoped she wouldn't press for more. "I guess we'll see."

Isa was silent. She stared out at the water. Adrian thought that she was imagining him with a tail, swimming among the waves.

"You have powers. You made the people at the party forget what you did that day, and you can communicate with fish."

"Yes," he admitted. "But I find my powers are

getting weaker the longer I stay on land. I can't even talk to Moona now."

The statement gutted him.

"Do mermaids get married?" Isa wondered aloud.

"We have mates," Adrian said.

"I bet your dad isn't happy you picked a human," she mumbled glumly.

"I don't care what my dad thinks." He grabbed her chin. "I care about us. I came on land to be with you. That's all that matters."

"How could you give up the entire ocean to be with me? I don't get it," Isa said. She looked frustrated.

"One day, you will." Adrian kissed her. "Can we stop talking about this? I don't want to mull over the past. That's behind me. I want to talk about what's ahead."

Isa seemed hesitant, but she said, "Okay."

The rest of the night was spent pointing out constellations, and Isa unsuccessfully trying to teach Adrian how to cook after both of them grew hungry for a late-night snack. Although he was relieved to get everything off his chest. Adrian felt like the pit of nervousness in his gut had grown larger rather than shrunk.

There was only one more day left. If Isa didn't tell him that she loved him by midnight tomorrow, he'd lose her.

This was his last chance.

CHAPTER FOURTEEN

ISA

Isa woke up the morning of the Seaside Ball in a sour mood.

She shouldn't have felt that way, because she'd woken on the beach. The sun was rising and Adrian was next to her, but still, there was an aching feeling in her chest that told her not to attend the ball.

Just stay with Adrian. Eat junk food. Go somewhere fun. Blow it off, her mind repeated over and over.

Every time she thought about the ball, she had this rotten feeling. It was like... her instincts were telling her to stay away.

She checked her phone. Already, there were a million texts from Shelly and Harbor about the ball and if she was going. She knew if she didn't show up, they would be disappointed. Not to mention her father would blow his top if he found out his daughter was a no-show at the premiere event of the year.

She still had to think about it.

Her mind was whirling with the reality that Adrian was a merman. This was too much information to take in. If merpeople existed, what other kinds of creatures were out there in the world? Did dragons, werewolves, and fairies exist, too?

Isa decided that for her, personally, she had hooked up with a merman, so she knew at the very least that merpeople existed. And no matter how Adrian had reassured her that this was permanent, she knew him being human had to come at a steep price. Despite his reassurance, she wasn't sure whatever Adrian had gotten himself into was over yet.

Isa had the idea that she and Adrian should go to Orlando. Enjoy the theme parks, go shopping— maybe do a bit of clubbing. They could avoid the Seaside Ball completely.

Her chest settled when she thought of this, and Adrian woke up beside her. He blinked a few times. Isa smiled when she saw his bright blue eyes spark as they settled on her face.

"Hey," she whispered. She bent down to kiss him. "How are you feeling?"

Adrian rubbed his chest. "A bit... *weird* to tell you the truth. I don't know why."

"Me too."

They stared at each other for a moment, then Isa said, "I was thinking we should go to Orlando.

It would be fun — we could even get a hotel for the night."

Or forever… and never come back.

"Sounds good." Adrian sat up. "You sure you don't want to go to the ball?"

Isa opened her mouth to respond, but then she heard, "Isa!"

She whipped her head around. Running down the shore were Harbor and Shelly.

Dammit. She should've *known* her friends would come looking for her at the beach.

"Woah," Harbor said when she noticed Isa's blue locks. "You want to look like an alien?"

"Hey," Shelly said, ignoring Harbor's rudeness, though she was staring at Isa's blue hair, too. "We came looking for you. You said we'd get ready for the dance together!'

Isa had never said such a thing, but she said, "It's the morning. The ball isn't until seven. It's too early to start getting ready."

"It's *never* too early to start looking good," Harbor responded. "Isa, you *promised* you'd come! Are you really going to back out now? Ditching us would be a really shitty thing to do."

She wasn't a fan of the guilt trip, but unfortunately, it worked.

Isa turned to look at Adrian. He stared back at her. "I'm okay with whatever you want to do."

Adrian truly meant it, but the pressure of what *everyone else* wanted got to her, and became overwhelming. So Isa gave up what she desired, and settled. "Okay. I guess I'll go."

Harbor and Shelly squealed, but the person she was inside was rotting. The voice within her screamed that this was a mistake.

"Come on," Harbor said. "I want to get a new lipstick. The shade I've got now doesn't match my dress."

"I'm busy today," Isa lied. "I'll meet up with you guys around four."

Her friends grumbled and groaned, and Harbor mumbled some- thing under her breath about Isa being obsessed with her new boyfriend, but Isa tried not to hear her.

Adrian nudged her shoulder. "So if you're going to the ball later, what do you want to do in the meantime?"

She threw her arms around his shoulders. "How does brunch sound?"

❧

ISA AND ADRIAN SPENT THE ENTIRE DAY PLAYING volleyball and chasing after the ice cream truck on the beach. It was fun, blissful. She almost forgot about the Seaside Ball.

But when she returned to her house at three, she felt like chains were being fastened to her ankles. How had she let her friends talk her into this?

"I'll stay down here and get ready," Adrian said.

"I can't wait to see what you look like."

Isa smiled. At least Adrian was going to see how pretty she looked, and she was going with him as her date. A ball was supposed to be romantic, right?

An hour later, Isa was looking for every excuse to get out of this. As Shelly piled her hair in a crown at the top of her head, and as Harbor dotted her face with makeup, Isa forced a porcelain smile.

She looked at herself in the mirror, and felt confident in her dress. But Harbor and Shelly immediately tore it down.

"There are *so* many sequins on this thing. I think I'm gonna go blind," Shelly said as she examined the blue dress. "Don't you think it's tacky?"

"What are you trying to be, a mermaid?" Harbor laughed. She threw a plain A-line dress in a light purple color at Isa. "Try this on. It was my prom dress, but *anything's* better than that thing Adrian bought you."

Isa did as she was told. She stood in Harbor's prom dress in front of the mirror, staring at herself. Her green eyes looked dead.

This isn't me, she thought. *This is who everyone wants me to be.*

Isa took off the spare, threw it aside, and said, "No. I'm wearing the dress I picked." If she was being forced to go to this stupid thing, she was at least wearing what she wanted.

Harbor and Shelly made faces as Isa slipped her blue mermaid dress back on, but Isa didn't care.

She shoved her feet in blue heels and made her way down the staircase.

Adrian was dressed in a slim navy tux that fit closely to his form. He grinned broadly as he watched her come down the staircase and took her by the arm. "Ready to go?"

"Let's get this over with," she breathed, glad of the feel of Adrian against her.

The Seaside Ball was held at an actual castle on the beach, on the far side of town. The castle had been a house for a general after the Civil War, but once the South lost, the general moved on and left the castle to Coral Bay. It was used mainly for conferences and weddings, but its biggest event of the year was always the Seaside Ball.

Everyone from Coral Bay was there, young and old. Children and elders alike mingled with the adults in the grand ballroom. The ceiling was made of glass and and fixed with crystal chandeliers. The house was decorated with the best handkerchiefs and china, round tables fitted with silk covers, ornate centerpieces of blue and green stones.

No expense was spared when decorating for the ball, and the citizens of Coral Bay knew it. Even Adrian seemed impressed.

When she was younger, Isa used to love the Seaside Ball— it was her favorite party of the year. But once people kept prodding her that she would soon be the next Queen, it became something she hated.

People were staring. They were whispering

about her blue hair, her outlandish dress. Isa caught a few girls laughing at her behind her back.

Adrian tugged her onto the dance floor. "Don't look at them. Look at me."

She did. Isa fixated her eyes onto Adrian's and pretended not to notice anyone else.

"It's better to be the center of attention than to blend in with the crowd," Adrian whispered. "They just don't like you because you have the courage to be different, and they don't."

The music started. Adrian had two left feet. Isa was okay at dancing, but Adrian kept stepping on her toes and making a bigger scene. They weren't going along with the dance properly, and it was clear that wasn't allowed.

"I don't think they approve," Isa said to Adrian quietly, privately delighted.

"I'm better with my fins," he whispered, and Isa laughed.

Her eyes flickered from Adrian's face to her high school friends, just for a moment. The laughter was gone now. Irritation had taken its place.

"They're pissed I'm having a good time." Isa smirked.

"Good. Let's make them angrier." Adrian kissed her on the lips deeply, in public. Isa could almost hear the shouts of outrage from here. Public displays of affection at the Seaside Ball were definitely forbidden. She loved breaking the rules.

Isa danced with Adrian until she could no longer, and dinner was served. She sat at a round table with Adrian, Harbor, and Shelly. Isa noticed her friends hadn't brought any dates, and seemed sour that Adrian was there.

They were served lobster, steak, and asparagus with mashed potatoes. Isa and Adrian didn't stop talking all through dinner, but Harbor and Shelly were unusually quiet.

Isa reasoned this wasn't so bad and the ball wasn't going as terribly as she thought it would. She was even having fun. Maybe it was a good decision to come here, and her earlier worries had been nerves.

During dinner, Shelly *accidentally* knocked over a glass of wine. It went spilling over onto Adrian's jacket.

"Oh, I'm so sorry!" Shelly said, and she dabbed at the spot on Adrian's jacket with a napkin. "I can fix this."

"Don't mind." Adrian smiled at her kindly. "I'll take care of it. Be back in a bit."

Adrian went to the washroom to clean his suit jacket. Isa's eyes followed him longingly as he left.

"Finally, he's gone," Harbor said restlessly as she threw down her fork. "We can talk."

"What do you mean?" Isa asked. "Anything you can say to me, you can say in front of Adrian."

"No, we can't," Harbor started. "Listen, Isa, we get that he's hot and all, but you're acting different since you met him."

"Different?" Isa asked.

"You're not the same. You barely hang out with

us anymore, and when you do, you're somewhere else," Shelly said. "It's like you're avoiding us!"

"Adrian and I just met. We've only been together a few days," Isa said slowly.

"Exactly!" Harbor burst. "You've been dating him less than a week, and it's like you're a completely new person. You're not the Isa we know at all! I mean, he even convinced you to dye your beautiful hair that stupid shade of blue!"

"He's *changing* you," Shelly said. "We don't like this new Isa you're becoming."

Isa realized something very sad then. She didn't actually *like* Harbor and Shelly. It wasn't that they were bad people... but they weren't her friends. Not really. If they did know her, they'd realize how important all of this was to her... her newfound self, her blue hair... Adrian.

Isa acknowledged they'd never had a deep conversation, never shared any common interests. Isa had gravitated toward Harbor and Shelly in college, because they were the popular kind of girls people *expected* her to have as her friends.

That wasn't fair. To herself, or to Harbor and Shelly. They deserved to have *true* friends who liked them for who they really were inside. Not fake-ass companions who merely hung around because they had nothing better to do. She'd pretended to like both of them, and gone along with whatever they wanted to do even if she wasn't interested, and beyond being false, it was cruel. She'd never given these girls a chance to know the real her, because she'd been too afraid to be authentic, and that was wrong. If she couldn't trust these girls not to judge her, she couldn't be friends with them.

She never should've spoken to them in the first place. And right now, she was going to correct that mistake.

Isa felt a steely ball of nerve rise up in her, and she said, "You don't have to like who I'm becoming. *I do.* And I'm not sorry if I'm not the person you expect me to be, but I can't lie to myself anymore about who I am."

Isa got up with such force from the table that it shook. She stormed off to find Adrian, angry that they could say such things to her. This was who she really was! She was trying to be better at being herself!

... But maybe that was her fault for being fake around them. They didn't know the real her. Adrian forced Isa to become her true self whenever he was around, because there was no way possible for her to be fake while around him.

Isa went toward the bathrooms, but before she could enter, she ran into someone in the hallway.

"Dad?" Isa gaped. There her father was, all dressed up in his military uniform. His expression was completely shocked as he took in her blue hair, her attention-grabbing dress.

She tried to gather herself as much as she could. "Dad, what are you doing here?"

"I wanted to surprise you. I didn't want to miss my daughter winning the Coral Crown," he said.

"But I didn't expect you to look like... *this*. Your hair is blue! And what in God's name are you wearing? It's embarrassing."

Isa swallowed. "I like how I look. I think I look pretty."

"You look like a slut," her father shot back. "If I had known you'd wear something like that, I would've never given you the money to pick it out yourself. It's disgraceful."

"You didn't buy this. My boyfriend did," she said lowly. "And for your information, *he* thinks I look beautiful."

Her father huffed. "I don't want to hear about another one of your boyfriends, Ria. They never last. His opinion doesn't matter. You're coming home with me this instant, and you're going to wash that blue dye out of your hair! Your mother would be ashamed if she knew you went out looking like this."

Her mother would be ashamed of Isa looking *like herself*, of looking like the person she wanted to be?

No. That was wrong. It crossed a line.

"My mother's the one who should be ashamed. *She's* the one who left me, so I don't give a damn what she thinks!" Isa yelled. "She's not here. And you should be ashamed, too, making me feel like shit when this is supposedly my night!"

"Come with me, *now*," her father growled. "This isn't who you are."

Isa shook her head. She backed away slowly, feeling horribly betrayed.

"This *is* me, Dad. This is who I am. It's too bad you weren't around enough to notice."

"Ria!" her father roared, but Isa took off. She didn't know if she wanted to scream or cry, but she did know she wanted to find Adrian.

She found him coming out of the men's room just outside the grand ballroom. The stain was gone, but water soaked the front of his jacket.

He noticed something was wrong as Isa flung herself into his arms. "Izzy, what's going on? What happened?"

Isa let one tear fall as she asked, "Adrian, do you love me?"

"What?" he gaped at her helplessly.

"Do you love me?"

This was something Isa had never done before. She'd never been vulnerable in this way. Guys always told her they loved her first, but it was just a way to get into her pants. She'd never said it back to anyone, not even Adrian.

And Isa knew in that moment she loved Adrian, but that she needed to hear him say it first. She needed to hear that someone out there cared about what she wanted— cared about who she was, and not just what they created her to be.

She needed to know this was real, and not a fairy tale.

But Adrian didn't give the answer she expected.

He let go of her and said slowly, "I... I can't say that."

The floor dropped underneath Isa's feet. She fell so far that she thought she was sinking into some sort of hell. "Why not?"

"I... I just can't."

"You don't love me?"

Adrian gazed miserably at her, void of any response.

Isa took it as her answer.

It didn't make sense. How could Adrian come on land for her, give up being a merman, give up *everything*, if he didn't love her?

Maybe everything he said to her was a lie and he didn't mean any of it.

Maybe this was all a prank and he wasn't a merman at all. She couldn't believe she'd been so stupid, and fallen for such a childish ploy.

"You're a liar, Adrian," Isa whispered. She tore herself away from him.

"Izzy, wait!" Adrian cried, but it was too late. Isa had heard enough.

She needed to get out of here.

This night was nothing short of a disaster. Isa was about to leave.

But as she was pushing her way through the crowd, she heard a voice call, "And this year's winner of the Coral Queen crown is... Isa Davis!"

Isa stopped cold. A million hands were on her back, and there were a bunch of smiling faces congratulating her. She noticed the expressions of the other girls steaming with envy. People pushed her toward the stage, and Isa's legs betrayed her as they obeyed willingly. Isa was forced to climb up on stage to accept the crown, forcing back tears.

"Told you," Brently said beside her. "I *knew* I was going to get Coral King. Where's your boyfriend?"

Isa had to turn her back on him to wipe away the tears. "Not here."

She left the stage before Brently took her response as an invitation, and before she had to give a speech. Several people tried to stop her, but she covered her face and ran out the door before they could.

Isa hurried to the beach. She kicked her heels off at the doors of the castle and left them there, running as fast as she could in her dress toward the place where the ocean met the shore.

She only stopped when she could feel the soft waves brushing up against her feet.

Isa took the crown off her head. She tossed it as far as she could into the sea, letting out a painful scream.

Her eyes caught the horizon line. Isa wanted to sink into that thin line and hide away, forever and ever.

The sea called to her. Not caring what happened to her dress, Isa wandered into the waves and closed her eyes, half hoping she'd drown. At least then, nobody would tell her what to do anymore.

As she entered the water, a pair of hands closed

over her mouth. Isa's eyes snapped wide open as a pair of tentacles wrapped themselves around her legs and arms, pinning them to her sides.

Isa tried to scream, but nothing came out. She heard a dark chuckle, and a sinister voice whispered in her ear, "Got you."

CHAPTER FIFTEEN
ADRIAN

Adrian had never felt more miserable in his life. He'd been *so close.* He could see it in her eyes when they were dancing earlier. She loved him. He *knew* she loved him, and she was about to tell him, but she wanted to know if he loved her first.

Something had upset her, that much was obvious. It wasn't like her to act this way. Isa was always composed. She never lost control.

Tonight was different. He saw something sickening in her eyes. She'd been wounded by someone she cared about— maybe a few people. Adrian wasn't sure how she could go from being fine to being completely devastated in the span of less than a few minutes, unless someone had truly wounded her.

But her rejection had done worse than break his heart— it had broken their connection. Isa refusing his love felt like a sharp board being snapped in half on top of his chest. Before, Adrian could feel her happiness, her joy, her pain and sadness.

Now, there was nothing. He could no longer sense her, and that frightened him. He was free to choose another.

Despite the mating bond being broken, Adrian was still madly in love with Isa. His feelings hadn't changed. He still felt like he would die without her. He'd wondered if his heart would choose differently once the mating bond was broken, and refused to think about it, but he had nothing to fear. Adrian's heart would always belong to Isa, no matter what magic did or did not bind it.

Fated mates or not, Stavros' spell was still holding. Adrian had some time before he would be forced to return to the sea. He had to find Isa, and make her change her mind.

"Sorry," Adrian said as he bumped into a man much larger than him. The man was wearing a Navy uniform. He instantly snapped when Adrian accidentally knocked him over.

"Watch where you're walking, boy," he growled. "You ought to be taught some manners."

Adrian was about to bite back a comment, before the man's eyes struck him. They were light green and churning like the sea.

Like Isa's.

It was *him*. He'd upset her. Her father had shown up and ruined everything. "Do you know where Isa is?"

The man's eyes narrowed suspiciously. "Why would I? After tonight, I've realized she's no daughter of mine."

Rage crashed within Adrian, and he snarled, "You better damn well tell me where she is."

The man sneered, "Or what? She ran off. Are you the new jackass she's dating?"

Adrian shoved him aside. He looked through the ballroom frantically, scanning the hundreds of faces in the crowd. Where was she?

He looked out a window and spotted Isa standing on the shoreline. He ran outside onto the beach and called her name, but before she could hear him, a figure rose out of the water.

"No!" Adrian screamed, but it was too late. Stavros wrapped his tentacles around Isa and yanked her downward, swimming out to sea. Adrian watched Isa's head bob along the top of the water as Stavros took her farther and farther into the ocean.

Adrian ran into the sea. He jumped against the waves and started paddling, swimming after Stavros with all his might. But the waves were too strong for a human to master, and Adrian was forced to turn back and watch as Stavros carried his love far away.

"No," Adrian wept. He knotted his fingers into his hair and pulled. Stavros had Isa. Who knew what he would do to her?

There was a bump against his leg. Adrian looked down and saw Moona's black eyes. She huffed and nibbled at his calves.

"I'm sorry, Moona," Adrian said mournfully. "I can't understand you."

Moona rammed herself into Adrian's side, and he nearly fell over. That got the message across.

"Right," he said. "I know what to do."

Isa had given Adrian her car keys to hold onto, since he was the only one with pockets. Adrian got into her car and drove to the docks. He broke a window to get into her uncle's office, and stole the keys to a boat. He hauled up the anchor, then drove the boat out to sea as fast as he could.

Moona kept up, to the best of her ability. When Adrian stopped the boat, he dropped anchor over the area where he knew Stavros' lair lurked.

Moona worriedly skimmed along the surface. By this point, the sky was dark and the moon was high.

It was then that midnight came over the earth, and Adrian was forced to change.

The agonizing pain came over him again. A fieriness came over his body. Every breath he took felt like knives piercing into his lungs. He tilted overboard, forced to return to the water. His legs were gone, and his tail was back. He could feel magic coursing through his veins strongly once more.

That was it. He'd lost the bargain. He'd never become human again.

A hollowness entered him, consuming him from the inside as he withered within.

It didn't matter. He had to save Isa, whether

they could be together or not. He wouldn't let her die because of a mistake he'd made.

But if the spell was over... Stavros ended up with nothing, didn't he? The deal was if Isa told Adrian she loved him, he'd remain a human forever, and Stavros would inherit the sea.

So what could Stavros possibly gain by taking Isa hostage?

Adrian didn't have time to think about it. He was didn't know where Isa was, but he was sure Stavros was in his lair, and he was waiting.

Moona swam by his side. He was able to understand her again as she asked, "What are you going to do now?"

Adrian sighed. "I'm going to do what I should've done in the first place. Ask for help."

He closed his eyes and spread his attention far and wide, throughout the water. He knew his father was listening. Poseidon *always* paid attention to the sea. Adrian called out to his father, begging for him to arrive.

By the time he opened his eyes again, Poseidon was there, appearing drastically worried.

"Adrian," Poseidon started. "Where have you been? Your mother and I have been worried sick about you."

His father was no longer angry. He understood he'd crossed a line during their fight.

Adrian bowed his head. "I'm sorry, Dad. I've finally learned I can't keep running away from my problems."

He cleared his throat. "I need your help. I'm in trouble."

"What kind of trouble?" Poseidon's eyes narrowed.

Poseidon's fingers tightened on his trident as Adrian explained. "I made a deal with Stavros. I bargained with him to become a human for three days so I could be with Isa... she was the human girl I told you about before. Stavros agreed that if she told me she loved me before the three days were up, I'd get to stay human forever."

Adrian looked down. "But it didn't work. She never said she loved me, and the spell broke."

"What did you trade for his magic?" Poseidon asked.

"I told him he could take my place as heir. I'm sorry," Adrian said as Poseidon frowned. "I wasn't thinking. But it doesn't matter. The deal is void, because it never happened. She never said she loved me."

"I see. But son, why would you go to Stavros?"

"I didn't have a choice, Dad. You didn't want to listen," Adrian said, and his voice cracked.

"Your mother convinced me I was too hasty in my decision. By the next morning, I was considering giving this girl a chance. But by that time, you were gone," Poseidon said.

"I've really messed things up, haven't I?" Adrian cringed, and Moona swam beneath his hand to comfort him.

"Not yet, you haven't. If the deal is broken, why are you still in trouble?"

"Because he took her, Dad." Adrian's tone was desperate. "He kidnapped Isa. Before, I was confident that I could beat him alone, but now I'm not so sure I can. Not without your help."

"I will always be here to help my son." Hot bubbles boiled from the tips of Poseidon's trident. "And I am tired of my younger brother meddling in business that is not his. It is high tide I teach him a lesson."

Poseidon opened his free hand, and Adrian's trident appeared within. He tossed it to Adrian.

"Moona, stay here," he told his friend. "This could get dangerous."

Moona said nothing, only bobbed. Poseidon and Adrian turned downward, swimming toward Stavros' lair.

"There is nothing to be afraid of, son," Poseidon said. "We're going to take care of this."

Adrian hoped so. He prayed that Isa was all right and that Stavros hadn't harmed her.

But, at the same time... there was a nagging feeling inside of him that Stavros had this planned. He *knew* Adrian would go to Poseidon for help. But why would Stavros be risky enough to tempt a god into war?

His uncle was either insane... or he was about to fool them all.

CHAPTER SIXTEEN
ISA

Isa could hardly believe this was happening. She had been kidnapped by a man who was half-man, half-squid.

"Let me go!" Isa cried. She struggled against her captor's grip at the surface, but even if she got away, there was nowhere for her to escape. She was in the middle of the ocean, and she couldn't swim through these waves, not miles back to shore.

"Calm yourself, mortal. My name is Stavros, and you are about to witness the transformation of a king," he hissed.

Stavros forced some sort of concoction down Isa's throat, then dragged her downward. The potion burned and tasted awful. Yet she found that with the help of it, she was able to breathe underwater, and she could open her eyes without the salt burning them.

At least he wanted her alive. She wasn't sure for what reason, or for how long that would be.

Stavros took her downward, to the very bottom of the ocean. He dragged her into some sort of cave, then tied her to a long, thin rock at the center of it. Isa screamed and struggled. Stavros ignored her as he began pouring potion upon potion into a large cauldron. The concoction exploded and changed colors with every ingredient he added.

"You're the one who made the deal with Adrian, didn't you?" Isa asked. "You changed him."

"You're bright, aren't you," Stavros said, and he rolled his eyes. "Yes, child, it was me."

"Why did you bring me down here?" Isa asked. "I don't understand."

"My girl, capturing you was the crucial part of the plan," Stavros told her sharply. "Now be quiet."

Isa's mouth wobbled. "Well, it doesn't matter. He wasn't in love with me, anyway. He's not coming to my rescue. He's just going to leave me here." Isa's tone had a measure of defeat to it.

"Of course he was in love with you, you stupid girl," Stavros sneered. "He practically threw himself at my tentacles, begging me to make him human so he could be with you. It was pathetic."

Isa's eyes widened. "But then... why wouldn't he tell me?"

"Because that was the condition of our agreement. You had to tell him that you loved him *first* for the spell to hold. If he said anything of the sort to you, the deal would be broken." Stavros tossed a flask casually aside, and it shattered on the cave wall.

A terrible pain dug into her, and Isa hung her head. She'd been so blind. A moment of irrational thought had ruined everything. All she had to do was tell Adrian she loved him, and she could've lived with him happily-ever-after.

But Stavros, for whatever reason, had been relying on the hope that she wouldn't confess her love. And she'd come through on that hope, that was for damn sure.

Stavros finished with the potion and faced the entrance of the cave. He was biding his time. Waiting.

Eventually, two figures came into view. Isa assumed one of them must be Poseidon; he was large and powerful, a merman that was twice the size of Stavros.

Isa's heart stopped as she recognized the person beside him. It was Adrian... but he looked different. Gone were his legs. They were replaced by a long green tail, with scales that shimmered like emeralds, and fins that moved as powerfully as the ocean itself. He carried a golden trident, and his red hair weaved beautifully in the water.

The sight of him— Adrian as he *truly* was, and not who he'd became for her— made her breathless.

When Poseidon and Adrian entered the cave, Stavros smiled. "Not so fast."

He swam behind Isa and pointed a knife of bone at her throat. "Come any closer, and I'll kill the girl. Or perhaps I'll kill her anyway, just to make it fun."

Adrian instantly turned pale. The water around Poseidon grew darker. "Don't dare to play games with me, brother. My patience has run out. Surrender now, and I won't take your life."

"This isn't a game," Stavros hissed. "I'm deadly serious."

Stavros stuck the point of the knife into Isa's neck, and she started to bleed. The knife wasn't like any other knife— it stung, and caused a pain like needles to spread throughout her body. Isa started to scream in agony. Stavros' smile only widened.

"Dad, please, do something!" Adrian shouted.

"Enough of this!" Poseidon roared, and Stavros drew the knife out from her skin. "What is it you ask for?"

Isa hung limply in her binds. This was the moment Stavros been waiting for. "My request is simple. Your crown for the girl. If you pass the sea onto me, your son's mate will be spared."

Poseidon didn't make a move, but neither did his expression change.

Isa looked between him, certain she was a goner.

"Dad..." Adrian whimpered.

Yet Poseidon's mind was already made up. He slowly floated toward his brother and offered his trident before him.

"I will do anything to spare my son more pain. It is one thing to end the fanciful crush of a teenage boy, another to ignore a mating bond. I will not break his heart." he said. Poseidon handed off his trident to his brother, then bowed.

The very sea trembled as Poseidon gave the ocean to Stavros.

"At last," Stavros breathed in one, long breath. He snatched the trident from Poseidon and clutched it tightly. "The sea is mine."

Stavros grabbed a flask, and scooped up the potion that was brewing within the cauldron. He drank it in one gulp, then tossed the glass aside. He laughed and laughed as his form began to change, morphing throughout the cave.

"Now all the ocean shall know of my power!" Stavros called triumphantly. Poseidon's trident shattered into dust as Stavros' tentacles grew larger and larger.

Adrian had the good sense to cut Isa loose. He grabbed her, and the three of them swam away as quickly as they could out of the cave and into the open ocean.

There was a shrieking sound, and the three of them turned around. A harsh, horrified yell emitted from Isa's throat at the monster she saw. The squid was gigantic, as large as a ship, with tentacles that trailed behind him a mile long. The tentacles weaved throughout the water, and a singular brown eye fixated on them as the squid's gargantuan beak snapped and clicked.

Stavros had become the kraken.

Adrian's arms were still around her. He swam

Isa to the surface. Above, the ocean had turned into a deadly squall. The waves were rough and hard, slamming Adrian and Isa back and forth. They were larger than even the wave she'd tried to surf, and angrier. Rain was pouring down from the sky in buckets. Thunder echoed and crackled, mixing with the lightning that was coursing across the sky. Gray clouds swirled above them, forming an eye with an open circle at the center.

Adrian threw her up onto the boat. The waves were so rocky that Isa had to hold onto the railing to avoid being tossed off.

"Take the boat and go back to shore before the storm destroys it," Adrian told her quickly. "I'll do what I can to stop him before the storm becomes a hurricane."

"I love you, Adrian." Isa fell to her knees and leaned over the boat to be closer to him, reaching out her hand.

"I know you love me. I love you, too," Adrian said. "But I can't leave my dad out here alone. This is my fault."

"Don't leave." Tears dripped down her face, mixing with the rain.

"I'm sorry, Izzy," he whispered. "I have to fix the mess I've made."

He kissed her hand in farewell, then dove back down. Isa's eyes frantically searched the water for Adrian, but she didn't find him.

"Dammit!" Isa clung to the railing and looked around. She couldn't head back to shore. She wouldn't. Not while Adrian was risking her life for her.

A few tentacles of the kraken rose out of the water, and Isa's heart skipped a beat.

She knew the anatomy of squids. She'd studied them at the aquarium, and in school. Squids had several central nervous systems, but there was only one that controlled everything. If Stavros was to be taken down, there was only one way.

Her uncle's harpoon was still hanging on the boat. Looking at the harpoon, Isa summoned her courage.

Isa pulled up the anchor. She then took down the harpoon, grabbed the wheel of the boat, and turned toward the kraken.

She wouldn't let Adrian face this alone.

CHAPTER SEVENTEEN

ADRIAN

Poseidon was helpless. He had neither his trident, nor his powers. Adrian was on his own.

Moona was nowhere to be seen. Adrian was glad; he wanted her to get out of here. This was no place for a manatee.

"Dad, stay back," Adrian told Poseidon. "I can handle this."

"Adrian, no!" Poseidon cried, but Adrian didn't listen. He swam forward, trident in hand toward the raging kraken.

Stavros was cackling. His laughter echoed and sent vibrations through the ocean as he floundered his giant tentacles about, utterly pleased with himself.

He saw Adrian approaching, and chuckled. *"What's this? You think you can still defeat me, boy?"*

Adrian didn't answer him, only jabbed his

trident in the direction of the kraken's tentacles. Stavros laughed harder, easily avoiding each stab. A tentacle latched onto Adrian's trident, ripping it out of his hands and tossing it to the ocean floor. The tentacle wrapped itself around Adrian's form, suction cups latching on. Adrian squirmed, but found himself unable to move.

Stavros squeezed. Adrian slowly felt the life being crushed from him as the tentacle wrapped tighter and tighter, preventing him from breathing, mashing his organs...

Then, in the distance, he saw a gray dot. Moona had returned— and she'd brought Celer, along with an entire army of merpeople, armed to the fins with tridents and spears.

At the sight of his rider being crushed, Celer charged. Celer smashed himself against the tentacle that was holding Adrian and bit down, hard.

As a reaction, the tentacle let go, and Adrian pried himself off of the suction cups. He climbed onto Celer's back, who swam downward. He reached for his trident on the ocean floor and rushed away before the tentacle could grab him again.

With the help of Celer, Adrian was faster than the tentacles. He outwitted Stavros' grasp and used his trident to stab into one tentacle, yanking it free from its host. He swung again, and another tentacle was severed. It dangled by a thread, causing blood to seep throughout the ocean.

"*Agh!*" Stavros squealed in pain at his severed

tentacles. The army had distracted the kraken, giving Adrian time to strike.

But as Adrian looked behind him through the red water, his heart thudded in his chest. The tentacles he'd just injured were healing, regrowing as if nothing had happened. Within moments, the damage Adrian had done was forgotten.

Now Stavros was angry. He reached out and grabbed multiple members of the army, opening his beak to consume them whole. Adrian was able to jab through the tentacle at the last minute, and everyone was able to swim free and escape. But like the others, the tentacle he'd cut through merely healed.

Even with all of them fighting against Stavros, he was still too powerful. No one could get close enough.

Adrian directed Celer around Stavros. He jabbed at the squid's body, and Poseidon directed the army to keep going for the tentacles, but no matter what injuries they dealt him, Stavros simply became stronger. The water was so red with blood it was turning a ruby color, but Stavros wasn't weakened.

Adrian looked above him and saw the tell-tale shadow of a boat far above. Panicking, he directed Celer upward, where the two of them crashed out of the water and onto the surface.

"Isa, I told you to go back!" Adrian roared over the sound of the storm.

"I'm not leaving you! We can beat this together!" she cried back.

"I can't let you get killed!"

"You have to trust me!" Isa screamed. "I have a plan!"

Adrian didn't want to put Isa in any more danger than she was already in. But if she had a plan, she was leagues ahead of the rest of them. "What do you want me to do?"

"Get him to the surface," Isa shouted. "I need him as close to the boat as possible!"

"Are you crazy!?" Adrian bellowed.

"Just do it!"

Necessity left them no time to argue. Adrian dove Celer downward, and he circled the kraken, trying to find an in.

The most obvious weakness Adrian could observe was Stavros' eyes, which were clearly exposed. Celer rushed forward and Adrian raised his trident, jabbing it into the left eyeball.

"*Ah!*" Stavros cried, more out of shock than pain. The trident had failed to puncture or wound the eyeball, but it turned red, so whatever Adrian had done had hurt.

A tentacle swiped by to knock him away, but Celer quickly spun, and Adrian jabbed his trident into the eye again.

"*Enough! Leave it alone!*" Stavros wailed. He swum higher, to get away from Adrian's sharp jabs.

The soldiers noticed that Adrian was chasing the squid upward, and they followed his lead. The mer-army took turns jabbing each eye and keeping the tentacles at bay, leaving Stavros unable to do anything but swim away, upward to the surface.

The kraken finally crashed through the surface, on the crest of a wave. It rocked Isa's little boat. Adrian had to hang on tightly to Celer to avoid being thrown off.

"Now what?" Adrian cried to Isa as Stavros floundered about, blinking his irritated eyes.

"Keep him busy!" All he saw was Isa's back. Adrian figured it was best to do as he was told and just roll with it.

"You heard the young lady!" Poseidon screamed. "Distract him!"

It took everything the soldiers had to get Stavros' attention. The minute they were sticking him in one place, they had to move to jab him in another, before one of Stavros' massive tentacles crushed them. Adrian looked for Isa. He noticed, with horror, that she was steering the boat toward the kraken.

Adrian wasn't quite sure what Isa was doing, but he knew he had to help. He cut ahead of the boat and chopped away at what tentacles he could, clearing a pathway for her.

Isa was next to the kraken's head now. She let go of the wheel and reached for something on the floor below her.

"Izzy, look out!" Adrian cried.

Stavros' tentacles wrapped around the boat and snapped it in two. Isa slid downward. She climbed up to the top of the boat, crawling onto the very tip in order to avoid sinking into the deep. Adrian saw her raise a large and rusty harpoon.

With all her might, Isa leapt from the boat and jumped onto the kraken, bringing the harpoon down. It pierced straight through Stavros' head.

Stavros screamed in horrible pain. His grip on the boat tightened, and Isa was propelled off of the kraken's head and into the stormy waves.

"Isa!" Adrian cried, and Celer whinnied.

The kraken's body twitched. Blood poured out from the wound where the harpoon stuck, and the wound didn't heal. Stavros' body went limp. His tentacles slid off the pieces of the broken boat as his body sunk slowly to the ocean floor in a massive heap.

He was finally dead.

The soldiers cheered, but Adrian didn't notice — he was looking for Isa within the crashing waves.

"Isa!" he called. He jumped off of Celer's back and swam in every direction he could.

He didn't see her. "Isa!"

"Over here!" He whipped around. Moona was supporting Isa and helping her swim against the rough waves, which were starting to calm down.

"Isa," he said again, as a finality. He picked her up and placed her on a piece of wreckage. Isa laid weakly on the board as the waves became calm again. The clouds cleared into a blue sky as the sun came into a new dawn, brightening the span of the sea with orange-yellow light.

It was finally over. But there was no facing the undeniable truth. She was a human, and he was a merman. They still couldn't be together, even after everything they'd been through.

"Adrian..." Isa started weakly. "I'm..."

He couldn't reply. There wasn't anything that he could say back except the cold, undeniable truth.

"Well, what do we have here?" Poseidon approached. As he opened his palm, a new trident formed, proclaiming him as king once more.

Adrian took Isa's hand and turned toward Poseidon. "Dad, this is Isa. My mate."

"Young lady, you were spectacularly brave out there," Poseidon said. "I don't know of any mermen, or merladies, that would've had half the courage to do what you just did."

"I thought all humans couldn't be trusted," Adrian said teasingly.

"Well..." Poseidon chuckled. "Not *all* humans."

"I had to do something, sir," Isa replied. "I couldn't let anything happen to Adrian. I'd never forgive myself. I... I wouldn't be able to live without him."

"Nor would I," Poseidon said gruffly. "And if there was any question of if you deserved my son, I think the question now is if he deserves *you*."

Adrian laughed. Isa tried not to blush.

"Sorry I don't look my best," Isa said. She played with the tatters of her soaking, ruined gown. "This isn't how I imagined meeting his parents would go."

"I think there could be a way to change that." Poseidon smiled. He dipped his trident downward, and through the water spread a light blue, sparkling magic.

The magic touched the edges of her frayed dress. It began to knit back together, but not into fabric.

It became a tail.

CHAPTER EIGHTEEN

ISA

Isa's eyes widened as the magic began to spread up her form. She looked down in amazement as her gown began to glow. "No way."

Things were quickly changing. Poseidon's magic modified her form, and Isa felt her legs knitting together into something new. Her dress melded to her body, sequins becoming sapphire scales and fins. The blue magic swirled all around her in a tornado, and Isa could handle it no longer. She dove off the board.

Isa put her hands in front of her in an arrow and swam through the water more quickly than she ever had. Her tail was powerful, propelling her through the sea faster than even a boat could sail. She swam for what felt like forever, joy and excitement coursing through her, unmatched by anything she'd ever felt in her entire life.

She ran her fingers through her wet locks. Her hair was still blue. She turned around to see Adrian and Poseidon had kept up with her. She did a back-flip in joy, spinning like a top within the ocean's depths.

"I'm a mermaid," she whispered, her childhood fantasy become reality. "A *real* mermaid."

Adrian's mouth was open. "Dad, you did this?"

"Of course I did," Poseidon said. "She has to be a mermaid if she's going to move to Aquatica and become your queen."

There was a pause. Adrian looked at Isa. "Do you *want* to move to Aquatica?"

Isa smiled slightly. "I don't know. What's it like?"

Adrian swam forward and took Isa's hand. "I'll show you."

A MORNING OF TOURING THE MERPEOPLE CITY had Isa hooked.

Everywhere she went, there was more to see. She had trouble taking in the fact that this was all real. There were hundreds upon hundreds of merpeople living in Aquatica, and the city was absolutely breathtaking.

Adrian's mother was more than welcoming… she felt like the mother Isa had never had. Ianthe wrapped Isa in a hug immediately the moment she saw her, before taking her aside privately. Ianthe discussed her job as the Mistress of the Waves, and told Isa what would be expected of her if she became Adrian's queen.

Ianthe was more than willing to take Isa on as her apprentice, but still, the task seemed daunting. Isa wasn't so sure she could do it, but Ianthe was certain she was up to the task.

Ianthe was supportive. Involved. It was more than her father ever had been.

Still, Isa hesitated. It was... a lot. A huge responsibility, that was for sure. Isa had always wanted to save ocean creatures as a marine biologist, but if she accepted the title of queen, she'd be able to save all of them. It would be her literal job, to safeguard the ocean from the dangers of humans and protect sea life from becoming extinct.

She just... wasn't sure if she was worthy enough.

Isa had the perfect time with Adrian. Yes, she wanted to stay here. But she wasn't sure if it was the right decision. She had school and responsibilities back home, not to mention her father. Could she really give that all up to become queen of the mermaids?

She wasn't going to lie, it sounded really tempting.

At the end of the day, Poseidon was looking expectantly at her in the throne room. "Well? Have you made your decision, child?"

Adrian's eyes were locked on her. The look he gave her was begging her to say yes.

Isa didn't know what to say. Poseidon wasn't the type of guy you told no.

Ianthe stepped in. "Perhaps she needs some time to think it over, dear," she said gently. "She has a life back on land, as well."

Adrian's face became crestfallen, and it hurt Isa. Poseidon rubbed his beard and said, "You're right. You are free to return to land, Isa— your legs shall reform, and you'll be able to become human for as long as you'd like. You too, Adrian. Stavros' spell is broken. You may now walk upon land anytime you wish. It is no longer forbidden for you to venture the human world. You may go there any time you please."

Adrian nodded. Isa reached out her hand to hold his.

"Come with me?" Isa asked Adrian. He nodded, and followed her out of the palace gates.

They swam through the ocean together, mostly in silence. Along the way, they bumped into Moona.

"Hi guys." Moona waved at them with her fin. "How's it going?"

Isa was ecstatic now she could understand her. "Oh, Moona." Isa hugged her. "You saved my life. Thank you."

"It wasn't anything." Moona shrugged, and she smacked Adrian with a flipper. "I'd do anything for this loser."

"Hey," Adrian said, and he narrowed his eyes.

Moona laughed. She waddled away through the waves, giving them the alone time they desired.

But before she left, Moona glanced behind her. "Isa… I hope you stay."

Adrian and Isa swam to the coral reef that they'd loved so much together and reached the surface. She could barely see the outline of Adrian's face in the moonless night.

"So…" he started. "What do you want to do?"

Isa sighed, and shrugged. "I don't know. I know I should stay on land. My dad needs me. I should remain human, and be a good daughter."

"What does *your heart* want you to do?"

Isa's fingers clenched Adrian's hands. "I was born to be a mermaid. I know I was. This one day has been more amazing than my entire life."

She stared down at the coral reef below. "I realize what I'm expected to do— to go home, take care of my dad, and be the polite, controlled woman I'm supposed to be. But it's not what I *want* to do. And I'm pretty tired of doing things for everyone else, but never for myself. This is my life. I need to live it in the truest way possible. I need to be me. And being a mermaid *is* being me."

"Does that mean you'll say yes?" Adrian's tone brightened.

"Absolutely." Isa laughed. "But I'll have to come back on land and make up some story for my dad. Tell him I'm transferring out of state or something. He won't care, not after our fight… and to be honest, after the way he spoke to me at the ball, I'm not sure if I want to see him again, anyway. I've only known your family for one day, but already, they care more about me than the people in Coral Bay do, and they've known me my entire life."

"It's a big deal to let your father go." Adrian frowned.

"I'm not giving up my family by making this decision— I'm *gaining* one. I've found someone who loves me, for me," Isa replied. "My choice is made. I want to stay with you."

"All right!" Adrian kissed her in ecstasy. "You're going to be my queen. *All mine.* You don't understand how incredible this is."

"What do you mean?" Isa tilted her head.

"I thought I'd never find the right girl. I figured finding someone would mean I'd be tied down forever, but it turns out, you're the biggest adventure of all, Isa. And I can't wait to explore you... every day, for the rest of my life."

"Aw, Adrian. That's so cute."

"Yeah, well." He grinned. "I'm a pretty good sweet talker."

Isa made a sarcastic noise, which turned into a tiny shriek of happiness. "I can hardly *believe* this. Mermaids are real, and I'm one of them! How amazing."

Isa sighed. "What else is out there? Peter Pan? The Big Bad Wolf?"

"I guess we'll never know." Adrian laughed. "Though someone might."

Isa smiled. She was counting on finding out.

"Come on, Adrian." Isa wiggled the sapphire

fishtail that she already loved so much. "Race you back to Aquatica."

THE END

What if Peter Pan was a girl? Find out in Lost: Twisted Fairy Tales Enchanted Fables, Book Two.

Turn the page to read the first chapter!

LOST
THE FIRST CHAPTER

There was nothing more Pan loved than running along the shore in her bare feet.

Except for, maybe, being chased by angry pirates. Her laughter soared over the darkening shore as she and the other Lost Girls fled into the jungle, careful not to drop their stolen feast.

"Enjoy your last meal, Pan!" a pirate from the queen's all-female crew screeched.

"We'll skin you alive for this!" called another.

"Why?" Pan yelled back at them. "Perhaps so you can wear mine instead of yours, you old hag?" She and her comrades slipped through a brush covered tunnel that none of the Pirate Queen's crew had any hope of following through with their gear. All Pan carried on her was a bronze dagger she'd found at the bottom of the cove. The small weapon hung at her hip, hiding among the fox tails and lady ferns adorning her skirt.

Pan had no fear of retribution. The Pirate Queen's crew hadn't found any of the Lost Girls' carefully selected hideouts in over a hundred years. Pan and her friends could continue to poach from them for the rest of their days as long as they moved camp every few moon cycles.

"It's almost getting too easy," Sprout said, crawling on her hands and knees behind Pan.

The tight tunnel was wafting with the scents of honey-roasted pig and spiced apples from the sack on her back. With game suddenly getting scarcer on the island and fruit mysteriously rotting on the vine, it had been ages since Pan had eaten something that hadn't been dried out and stored in the makeshift cellar at camp. Her belly roared with anticipation.

"They shouldn't have been so easily distracted," Pan said, already imagining licking the grease from her fingers. "When will they learn?"

A giggle echoed through the dark dirt walls. "Did you see the way they all jumped when they heard the fake ship's bell?" Sprout laughed. "Like they were going to get their hides whipped because The Pirate Queen had returned and they weren't all there to stand at attention!"

Thistle groaned. "Minerva's not going to like this. Her crew is just as hungry as we are. I bet when she hears of this, she'll find us and set fire to our beds while we sleep."

"And probably eat us, too," Briar chimed in.

"You all worry too much," Pan said. "Minerva

hasn't stepped off that ship in a century. She isn't going to break a sweat over a silly pig."

"Still…" Thistle said hesitantly. "We shouldn't light a fire tonight, since camp is so close to shore, and we already have a cooked meal."

Fauna shivered and whined, "I'm always cold when we don't light a fire."

"You can sleep next to me," Flora, her twin, offered, "but I'm not sharing my blanket."

"I don't want to sleep next to you," Fauna said. "Your farts smell like boar's breath."

"Say that again and I'll make you smell like something worse!"

Fauna huffed. "Like what, your stinky clam?"

Flora sent a donkey kick into her sister's shoulder. "You're lucky it's too tight in here to turn around, Fauna, or I'd punch you in your rotten tit!"

Pandora stopped crawling once they reached the opening. Sprout knelt behind her. Together, they waited for the twins to stop bickering.

"I heard some pirates talking at the beach," Sprout told Pan. "They're taking a trip to the mainland. I bet they'll have all kinds of strange food when they get back."

Pan grinned. "And we'll steal that, too."

She pushed back the ivy tendrils concealing the end of the burrow and greeted the open air with a stretch to her tip toes after climbing out. Dirt matted her bare knees and clung to her dress. She was careful not to disturb the dried poppies on her

MEGAN LINSKI

bodice or the foxtails hanging from her waist as she brushed herself clean.

Outside the tunnel, the waning moon rose over the grove of ruins the Lost Girls called home for the warm season. Hidden behind the grotto, the once towering stronghold now lay in crumbles beneath overgrown vines and layers of moss. What was left of the stone walls kept the girls cool in the day and was a stage for dancing shadows at night. The hideout was, by far, Pandora's favorite on the entire isle of Neverland. She loved drifting to sleep on the soft moss while listening to the songs of the nocturnal squabble monkeys.

Some nights, at witching hour, the sparkling chimes of a lone fairy would wake her and she'd sneak off to collect the excess pixie dust that sprinkled from their wings. She saved the pinches of magic in a pouch she kept on her belt and used it only in dire need—like when she needed to levitate a juicy pear off a pirate's plate.

Pan adjusted the sack of food on her shoulder and began the short descent down the cliff overlooking the hideout. Just as the sole of her foot reached a supporting rock, something thudded into her side, causing her to lose her grip and fall backward to the ground. Pan landed with a *thud* on top of the stolen pig.

When she opened her eyes, stars stared down at her. Sprout and Thistle called to her from the tunnel's opening. A streak of sparkling light blazed across her vision.

Pan sat up and cursed. "Tinkerbeau!"

The streak of light stilled to a soft glow, taking the form of a tiny man, panting as he pushed his sand-colored hair out of his green eyes. His trousers, made from last season's meadow weeds, sat wrinkled and tattered at his calves. His iridescent, pointed wings flitted as he hovered in the air, gleaming like starglass.

"For the umpteenth time, watch where you're going," Pan said as she stood and brushed herself off for a second time. "You knocked me over and nearly ruined our hard-earned feast."

Tinkerbeau seemed to pay her no mind, bobbing up and down in urgency. To almost everyone else, the fairy's voice sounded like the chime of a tiny bell, but Pan had spent enough decades with the fairy to understand Faerian with ease.

"What is it?" she asked, her tone on the edge of worry. She observed the pallor of his complexion, almost translucent from using too much of his pixie dust. "You've been flying," she realized. "Far, apparently. Where have you been?"

Tinkerbeau dinged as he twirled in a circle and pointed to the portal in the sky on the western shore of Neverland.

Pan glanced toward the swirling vortex of stars. "You've been to the human realm? Didn't I tell you to keep watch with the other girls?"

The fairy nodded. He tugged on Pan's wild copper hair, frivolously trying to pull her in the portal's direction.

"You want me to go back there with you?" she asked.

Tinkerbeau released her and nodded again, causing a bit of glittering dust to spill out of his hair.

"Now?" she whined. "I'm starving. Can't it wait until morning?"

The fairy's face burned red as he tugged on her again. Pan swatted him away as the other Lost Girls came down safely from the rocks.

"Is the food okay?" Fauna snatched the sack from Pan. She tore it open. After inspecting the meat, she grabbed a chunk of the roast pig and attacked it with her teeth.

"Not too bad," Fauna mumbled through a mouthful. "A bit squished from your fat ass, but it'll be all right."

"Give me that!" Pan ripped the sack from Fauna. "You know the rules. If you're so hungry, hurry and get to the others so we can *all* eat."

Fauna stuck out her tongue, but ultimately resigned, linking arms with her sister and marching into the brush.

Before Tinkerbeau could try to distract her from her meal again, Pan followed the other girls through the thick grove to their seasonal abode. The best any of them could guess was that the two and a half corner walls, along with a dilapidated antechamber, were once an apothecary. A cast iron cauldron still stood in the middle of the chamber, and shards of pottery and glass vials guarded the entrance. Anyone wishing to cross over the crumbling threshold had to be careful not to step on the trap. That, and Pan's nocturnal fairy companion, was their only means of defense against predators in the night.

The other Lost Girls had been waiting for Pan, greedily eyeing the grease-stained sack slung over her back. Briar, Pokeweed, and Clove had stayed behind to guard the camp. Pan noticed the floor had been swept, and the table had been cleared in hopes there would be a meal brought back to place on it. Without a word, Pan slammed the sack down on the table and cut the cloth sides with her dagger, spilling the meat and glazed apples onto the table in mouthwatering morsels. Briar and the other Lost Girls gasped as Thistle added fresh crackers and a jug of strawberry moon wine they'd saved for three seasons to the feast.

The Lost Girls didn't wait to dig in. They ravenously shoved pork in their mouths and licked the juice from their fingers. Within minutes, everyone's smiles glistened with grease and crumbs. Just as Pan was reaching for a leg, a chilling male voice froze her in her place.

"Pandora, Chieftain of the Lost Girls..."

She slowly turned to find a long-haired centaur looming behind her, arms crossed over his broad, smooth, chest. She knew that chest. How many summer nights had she pressed against it, moaning as the centaur's thick fingers explored the depths of the warm tunnel between her legs?

Pan trembled at the memory of it.

The centaur's voice was anything but warm as he declared, "You have been summoned by the Council. You must come with me."

Read the second book in the Twisted Fairy Tales shared universe, Lost by Constance Roberts, and continue the adventure!

About the Author

Megan Linski is a USA TODAY Bestselling Author. She is the author of more than fifty fantasy and paranormal novels which feature themes of friendship, community, and healthy romantic relationships. She has over fifteen years of experience writing books alongside working as a journalist and editor. She graduated from the University of Iowa, where she studied Creative Writing.

Her passions include ice skating and horseback riding. In her free time she enjoys dancing in the snow and drinking fancy coffee while at her natural habitat, the mall.

Megan advocates for the rights of the disabled, and is an activist for mental health awareness.

Megan co-writes the Hidden Legends Universe with Alicia Rades. She also writes under the pen name of Natalie Erin for the Creatures of the Lands series, co-authored by Krisen Lison.

You can find out more at www.meganlinski.com.

Made in the USA
Columbia, SC
23 June 2023

18754025R00129